JOE FROM WINNIPEG
ALL MY BEST

JOE FROM WINNIPEG ALL MY BEST

IAN ROSS

Joe from Winnipeg: All My Best
first published 2004 by
J. Gordon Shillingford Publishing Inc.
©2004 Ian Ross

Cover design by Doowah Design Inc.
Cover photo by David Patrick Armstrong
Author photo by Kathy Long
Printed and bound in Canada

We acknowledge the financial support of the Manitoba Arts Council, The Canada Council for the Arts and the Government of Canada through the Book Publishing Industry Development Program (BPIDP) for our publishing program.

Canadian Cataloguing in Publication Data

Ross, Ian, 1968–
        Joe from Winnipeg: all my best/Ian Ross.

ISBN 0-920486-78-9

I. Title.

PS8585.O84014J643 2004   081   C2004-906580-7

J. Gordon Shillingford Publishing
P.O. Box 86, RPO Corydon Avenue, Winnipeg, MB Canada R3M 3S3

Contents

Introduction

Meegwetch for reading this book, or at least parts of it. It's been an enriching experience writing and performing Joe from Winnipeg over the past six years. Choosing the various pieces that would be in this collection was also a lot of fun, a bit of a jigsaw puzzle, really, and some of the pieces I would like to have had in the book I just couldn't find. As my life got more chaotic and less routine, I found myself writing Joes in hotel rooms and e-mailing them to myself or Tom (Anniko, my producer at CBC Radio) or writing them longhand. I saved all of them, because I am from Winnipeg and a pack rat. I suspect there are more of us in Winnipeg than any other Canadian city, a hidden shame or strength, depending on how you look at it. One of the joys of going over the Joes that I wrote for radio and television was seeing how they evolved. I am not as fond of the later pieces, but that is probably because it was a difficult time in my life and I see some of that reflected in the commentaries. Joe seems a bit more angry, less forgiving and unhappy, which was how I was feeling at the time. I'm proud to say that I've since turned that around and am better than my old self. Please don't mind some of the weird spellings, as I sometimes wrote Joe phonetically, which tended to get out of hand, and now that I think about it, a bit strange, since I was the only one reading them and knew how I was going to pronounce the words. I'll always remember one morning having Janice (Moeller), who recorded me often, gently suggest that the piece that morning sounded "a bit too Joe." Is that possible? What's up with that?

My favourite piece is the one about yams, probably because it seems to capture all the things I've enjoyed about doing Joe from Winnipeg: some commentary on what was happening at the time, a story is being told, hopefully something is being taught about

Aboriginal perspectives, I find it funny, and it seems to make people feel good. All the things that I liked about doing Joe from Winnipeg.

I really do have to thank the many people who helped me with Joe and to bring him to life. Of course, my friend Tom Anniko, without whom none of this would have happened or been possible. I can't thank this wonderful man enough, for his courage, patience and, most of all, friendship. My publisher, Gord Shillingford, who changed my life by teaching me that words can be made into books. I have to thank all the people at CBC that have helped—Janice Moeller, Terry McLeod, Cecil Rosner, Wilma Chartrand, Kinsey Posen, Sonja Arab, Ray Bourrier, everyone I ever pulled away from their desk to record me, Brian Roundtree, my family and friends, Kerri and Julia, and Joe from Winnipeg's namesake, Joe Dudych. I'll tell that story. I showed up at the CBC with my first Joe from Winnipeg piece and was awaiting my actor, who didn't show up. Tom Anniko asked me if I could read, meaning could I act. I said yes, and he put a big hand on my shoulder, led me upstairs and put me in a recording studio. I began to pace, freaking out, realized I was pacing and sat down. I asked Tom if I could change any of this, meaning my script, and he said, "Of course, it's yours." So I looked at the character's name, which was Lenny, and since I wasn't Lenny, I needed a new name, so I asked the technician sitting beside Tom, who was fiddling with buttons and levels and things, and asked him what his name was. He looked up and said, "Joe." And I said, "Joe. Good enough." And I changed the character's name to Joe. As for what's next for Joe, I'm sure we haven't heard the last of him. I still like him, and others seem to as well, so hopefully what the character did for me and others can carry on in some way. And many deep and grateful thanks to everyone who listened and allowed me to have this gift for so many years. Meegwetch.

Ian Ross
November, 2004

Lemon Meringue Pie

Hey you guys. This is me, Joe from Winnipeg, Manitoba. I'm gonna be talkin' to you today about lemon meringue pie. My favourite. Just the other day, I was visiting my "community." Apparently we're not supposed to say "reserve." Now it's "community." What's up with that? A reserve by any other name would smell the same. Anyways. I'm visiting some of my family and I kind of got sick out there. Boy, I'm lying around convulsing, when all of a sudden my auntie brings me in a couple of pieces of pie. She never was all that good with fractions, and she ended up cutting me one piece about a fifth, and another about one seventh. And I'm eating my pie, and I'm looking at this one piece, and there were these little beads of something on the meringue part. Now I don't know if that's meringue oil, or condensation or what it is, but it's safe to eat. But I look at this sandy coloured, sweaty meringue and I think of sand. And sandbags. Which I was doing out at the "community." Making a few extra bucks. Anyways. I realize that my auntie's being extra nice to me. She made this pie, special. Just for me. And it's 'cause I'm sick that she's being nice to me. And I think about it. And you know, the only time some people are really nice to you is when you're sick. Now what's up with that? So, back to sandbags. There's gonna be the flood of the century here. I should say it's already happening. There's people complaining about being forced from where they live. And some people don't complain. They just pack up their lawnmowers and other things worth saving and are displaced persons for a while. So I'm on the bus, and this man starts talking to me about how deep the water is in his backyard. And I have to say I was a bit shocked. Normally people don't talk to me on the bus. Some people attract conversationalists, but not me. Except this one time. And this man is very polite. And pleasant. And talking about the weather. And how we both hate it. There's something good about talkin' about stuff you can't control. And I start telling this man about how I was sandbagging up at the "community," and I realize he thinks I'm talkin' about some kind of cult, because I keep saying the word "community." So I give up and start saying "reserve" and we're both even happier. Anyways, I'm talking about sandbagging the chief's house, a beautiful riverfront property near the powerlines. And he tells me that he's been volunteering to sandbag here in the city. Boy did I feel guilty that I was paid to sandbag, but I'd do it for free. And then we talk some more. Complain some more. And I tell him that every culture seems to have a flood story, and he asks me what the Native one is. And I tell him that it has to do with punishment I think, although I might be mixing up Noah in there, and that Nanabush and all the animals were stuck on a little raft. And Nanabush needed some earth, which was underneath the water, so that he could make the land again. So all the strong swimmers try. Like Otter and Beaver and those guys. But they all go down deep, deep, as deep as they can, but none of them can get to the bottom. So then Muskrat says, "Let me try." And they all laugh at him, but he does it anyways. He jumps in and he's gone a long, long time. And then. This is the sad part. His little body floats up. And the animals are all sad, but when they pull Muskrat onto the raft they see that in his little paw there's a clump of earth. And Nanabush uses that to make the land. "That's beautiful" says this sandbagger to me. And I say "Yeah." And after he gets off the bus, I think, why is that, that all cultures have a flood story? Maybe they all came from Grand Forks and Winnipeg. And then I think, hey, people usually complain about or hate the Americans, but now they're letting them stay at their houses 'cause of this flood. And then I'm thankful in a way. For this flood. Thankful that the weather, with blizzards and tornadoes and floods, can still let people talk to each other. Still treat each other like human beings. But like my auntie's lemon meringue pie, it has to get pretty bad before we're nice to each other. Again I ask you, what's up with that? This is Joe from Winnipeg. Meegwetch.

Baloney Sanwiches

Hey you guys. This is me, Joe from Winnipeg, Manitoba. I'm gonna be talkin' to you today about baloney sanwiches. My second favourite. My favourite's grilled cheese corned beef. Anyways. The other day I started sandbagging here in the city. All over the place. Wellington Crescent. Another crescent street just called Crescent. And even in St. Boniface on Taché. So I just get to Taché and I'm pretty hungry by then and I see that everyone's eating, but I tell myself that I can't eat yet 'cause I hadn't done any work there yet. I didn't want everyone to think I was some guy just comin' for a free lunch without doin' no work. I always heard there's no such thing as a free lunch, but with sandbaggin' there kind of is. So I hang around watching everyone eat until they start sandbaggin' again and I join in. And after we finish that load of sandbags off, some of us get to eat, so me and this other guy who I just met, Serge, start talking while we eat our sandwiches. And he's afraid to eat his sanwich 'cause the baloney looks a funny colour to him. Kind of like, pale grey. And I tell him that it's still good. "Baloney sometimes looks funny but it still tastes good." And especially this kind, which had a little bit of mustard on there. Mmmm. My second favourite. Anyways, we talk about the flood, and some people not being ready yet, even though there's lots of water already. So I tell him that it's like the time I had company coming and I had to prepare for four guests, but I didn't know what to do. So I went to Solo and picked up some bung balogna (I think that's different from baloney, more classy or something) and come home and fry some up for them, along with a nice macaroni in a cheese sauce. But wouldn't you know it, I tell him, two of the guests bring their partners, Boy, that's crazy. You know the first time I heard that I thought this couple was in business together, not living common-law. Anyways, I only had enough bung balogna for one more person. It was the end piece, that kind of looks like a convex lens. Or is it concave? Anyways, you can't cut this last piece properly without cutting your fingers, and it's too thick to make a sanwich with. So I ended up having to go without, and even then I barely had enough. Serge nodded his head, 'cause he knew what it was like, and he tells me he had the same situation when he made Cornish hens for his guests and one extra person showed up. How come extra people seem to come when you don't really need them, but not when you can use them sometimes like sandbagging? What's up with that? Anyways, what's a Cornish hen I ask him. And he says, "That's like a little chicken." Oh. So I start thinking about little chickens and wondering what they'd taste like in a sanwich. And then I think of Chicken Little. That little chicken who tried to tell everybody that the sky was falling. Except it already did fall here in Manitoba. All winter. And even a bit this weekend, it rained. And there's been some Chicken Littles around telling people this flood was gonna be REALLY bad, but no one listened, eh? Some still aren't. Come to think the same thing happened to Noah when there was a big flood. I guess there's something about floods that make us deny anything'll happen. Kind of like when we're young. I found it kind of funny too, that disaster times seem to be when some people believe what politicians tell them. Anyways, I wanna thank all you people who make sanwiches and sandbag and everyone who's helping. And everyone else who can, but aren't. Again I ask you what's up with that? This is Joe from Winnipeg. Meegwetch.

Lasagna

Hey you guys. This is me, Joe from Winnipeg, Manitoba. Today I'm gonna be talkin' to you about lasagna. My new favourite ethnic food. It used to be bannock and sausage, but I'm not sure if it's still ethnic, if you're part of that ethnic groupage. Ethnic groupage? What's up with that? Anyways, as you all know, there's this big flood that's happening here. So, just the other day, me and this guy, Serge, were goin' home after doing whatever we could to help these people near the Assiniboine River. And all of a sudden, we hear this, "hey." Someone calling out to us eh? It was funny, 'cause both of us, our first reaction was to jump. And even me, thinking I did something wrong. 'Cause whenever someone yells "hey" at you it usually means you screwed up or they're mad at you. What's up with that? Anyways, this nice woman invited us into her house to eat. And we both said "Sure." Right away. And this, nice, kind-hearted, soon-to-be ex-stranger. Fed us. Me and Serge. And she fed us this lasagna. With different kinds of cheese I can't pronounce the name of, and even raisins in there. I've only ever eaten raisins out of a box or a pie before. And REALLY good beef. Anyways, I tell this woman, Sarah, that I haven't eaten like this since I was a boy on the "community." I mean reserve. And she says, "Oh, do they eat lots of lasagna on the reserve?" And I say, "No. I mean being invited into someone's house, who I don't really know, to eat, and even then it was usually only at Christmas." And she was very humble. Saying, Iit was nothing." But all the while, I'm thinking, "What's up with this?" It's SO great. And then I start babbling. Poor old Serge didn't even get a chance to say nothin'. Anyways, I'm talkin' about the raisins, and cheeses and the beef. And how that I haven't tasted beef like that since I had to tenderize a steak with a balpeen hammer, 'cause my mallet was busted. And she laughs and we all laugh. And then I tell her about the time I got a twenty-pound sledgehammer dropped on top of my head. Boy, that was crazy. It just felt like my whole body went numb-like. But it was my own damn fault for not having my hardhat on. And you know, I remember laying there, with everyone looking down at me. And I'm thinking, what are you guys doing? Help me out here. And I felt really alone. And I thought about all the times I've been hurt, or incapacitated and sometimes laying there and people looking down at me, and me wishing it was them, or that I was the one looking down on everybody, and I felt really alone. And after Serge and me left, I kept thinkin' about this province. My favourite. And its people. And even this country. Also, my favourite. And its people. And how that for all you people out there who lost your homes, and your possessions and things. To remember. It's not like you're laying on the ground there alone. There's lots of people who are with you. Lots of people. And you know, usually when I say, "what's up with that?" I'm talkin' about something bad, but lately, I find I'm saying, "what's up with that?" like I'm all surprised, 'cause every day I see something different. That's good. Neighbours and strangers helpin' each other. With food. Clothes. Places to stay. Or sometimes even company. And you know, this'll be the last thing I say, we shouldn't have to say, "what's up with that?" when we see people being good to each other. And like the licence plate say, Manitoba is "friendly," and when it's in trouble it's good to know we have many friends. This is Joe from Winnipeg. Meegwetch.

Shortbread Cookies

Hey you guys. This is me, Joe from Winnipeg, Manitoba. I'm gonna be talkin' to you today about shortbread cookies. My alltime favourite. Especially the kind that are cut into the shapes of Christmas trees or Santa Clauses, with the coloured sugar on there, either red or green. How come we can't get that during the rest of the year? And you know, I'm even happy if they're just the plain kind with a piece of dried-up cherry on there, like Suzie Monias makes up there at Dauphin River. One time I even chipped a tooth on that little rock cherry. They were having this bake sale up there to raise money. And I ask Suzie, "Hey, how come you're always using dried-up cherry for your shortbread cookies? What's up with that?" And she says, sometimes she has to use little bits from old fruit cakes left from Christmas. And then I say, "Oh, so you're just being cheap then." And she says, "No. I'm recycling. And hey, at least I did something." I'm thinkin', boy, that's crazy. Why would someone try recycle fruit out of Christmas cakes? I know they're one of those things you either love them or hate them. Kind of like those purple gum, called Thrills. They either taste really good to you. Or else they taste like soap. I figure Suzie must be someone who hates Christmas cake, otherwise she wouldn't be hangin' onto them 'til late April. Early May. Anyways. Speakin' of thrills, that's what I gotta say these past weeks have been here in Manitoba. Scary thrills, thanks to Mother Nature. And even heart-warming thrills, thanks to true human nature. I'm not gonna tell you another flood story. It's still not over, but now that people are goin' back home, a lot of them have got one heck of a mess to clean up. And cleaning up's not fun. So I'm gonna ask you something here. I know, you're prob'ly saying, Joe's s'posed to be commentating, not asking. But right now, there's lots of people who still are in need. There's the Red River Relief happening now. And when I was thinkin' about ways to ask you to help out, be it money, or even just yourselves, and I know so many of you have already given, I thought boy, oh boy, what are you gonna do, Joe? Guilt trip them maybe. Nahhh. Beg them maybe. Nahhh. There's lots of my people doin' that already. Get smart, I told myself. But you know what? All I could think, was to just ask you. Gi bu go sa ni mi tin. That's in my language. Or else there's donnez s'il vous plait. Or else just, "please give." You know, that's a funny thing. Those words sound different, but they mean the same. And I don't know about you guys, but I'm a different person after what I've seen and been through. And like old Suzie Monias said, "At least I did something." And I know, those of you who did do something, will do a little more. And those of you who maybe didn't, now's the time. To all my fellow Canadians, Manitobans, Winnipeggers, and strangers who are now my friends. Meegwetch. Merci. Thank you. This is Joe from Winnipeg.

Thanksgivin'

Hey you guys, this is me, Joe from Winnipeg. Today I'm gonna be talkin' to you about my favrite holiday. Thanksgivin'. The one where we give thanks, and I doan know why we don't call it Givinthanks. What's up with that? It musta been from a French word or something, you know how some of their sentences are backwards in English, eh? Or I guess their forwards to them. Whatever. Maybe it means thanks for givin' us the land. Anyways, I gotta admit to somethin' I'm not s'posed to be proud of here. Lookin' in someone else's medcin cabnet and lovin' the Carpenters. I was helpin' fix my friend Jerry's sink in the bathroom. He figures 'cause I used to clean washrooms at the bus depot I must know how to fix 'em. I don't. Neither does he. We ended up strippin' one of the pipes and crackin' that heavy thing on the toilet you got to lift off whenever it don't flush right. I guess you're not s'posed to stand on it. Plus he insulted me likin' the Carpenters. 'Specially "On Top of the World." Boy, insultin' someone's music is like sayin' they got an ugly baby. You just shouldn't do it. Anyways, Jerry went to call the plumber and I ended up havin' to wash my hands in the bathtub 'cause the sink was really out of commishon. So, here's the part I'm not proud of. I foun my hand goin' for the medcin cabnet, eh? Boy, you know I don't know what's up with that? Me wantin' to look in other peoples' medcin cabnets. 'Cept I always get scared 'cause I think someone's gonna walk in on me at any moment, eh? An' I am invadin' someone's privacy. 'Cept I tell myself it's OK 'cause they could look in my medcin cabnet if they wanted to. If I had one. I only got one of those metal things to hold a cup and a plastic hamburglar I got free, to hold my toothbrush. Boy, you know, change your toothbrush every so often, or else it ends up lookin' like a bad haircut. Anyways, Jerry didn't have much intrestin' stuff in his medcin cabnet. No weird medications or nothin'. But he did have a monthly breast self-examination pamphlet. An boy, that's a good thing to have. But Jerry's single and got no girlfriend eh, so…what's up with that? Anyways, Jerry didn't have no money to pay me, but he said, "Here Joe, have some pie." He got a deal on pumpkin pie and he gave me one out of the six that he had. "Gettin' ready for Thanksgivin'?" I asked him. "I guess so. I forgot. I don't ushely celebrate it," he says to me. Not since his sister died, he tole me. "I'm sorry," I says. An tole him he could come celebrate Thanksgivin' chicken with me an my famly an friens. "Thanks. I'll do that." Boy, next to Christmas, Thanksgivin's my favourite. An you know, the thing I love about it, is that it was invented by the 'Nishnawbe and the White people. Although, I wish I had another way of sayin' that. White people sounds stupid. An you know, I think the reason why we made Thanksgivin' a holiday was 'cause our ancestors knew what we might be like for us today. Drivin' our four wheel drives an havin' alarm clocks that ain't roosters. An all that stuff we call modern convenience. An modern life. So busy, that we gotta remine ourselves to give thanks. Somethin' we should be doin' every day for all kines of reasons. There's lots to be thankful for. An for those of you who hear this an maybe you just lost someone you love. I know how hard that is, 'cause I've lost too. Everybody has. Or will. Be thankful you had them in yer life. An you got to know them. But anyways, I could fill up this whole time with things I'm thankful for, from bein' able to help bust someone's toilet (not on purpose) to eatin' pumpkin pie. An you know what? I like the Carpenters. An I'm not ashamed of it. An I don't want to feel like I gotta apologize about something that's sweet. An good. Boy, that felt good. Anyways, my thanks to the Creator for creatin' us. An for givin' us food to eat. An mouths to eat with. An talk with. An say, "Meegwetch, to you listenin' and all my friens. Thanks for bein' my friens." An especially, for the Carpenters. This is Joe from Winnipeg. Meegwetch.

Budget Surplus

Hey you guys, this is me, Joe from Winnipeg. Today I'm gonna be talkin' to you about the economy and this budget surplus thing that's s'posed to happen. I thought I'd talk about some good news for a change, since we're always hearin' about sad stuff or else how there's not enough money for this or that. But hey, it kine of sounds like this time there's gonna be a little extra money. But I doan wanna jinx it this surplus thing or nothin', 'cause when it comes to money I ushely get superstitious. I guess that's 'cause whenever I get extra money it comes from a little gamblin' on a scratch an win ticket or somethin'. You know I never won more than two bucks on those things. What's up with that? I s'pose I should be happy with doublin' my money. But anyways, I'm all thinkin' about the economy 'cause I ran into my frien Bernie. I ran into him yesterday and he's all happy, eh? "What's up, Bern?" I says to him. "I'm goin' to buy a fridge, Joe," he tells me. Right away I get kine of jealous, eh? 'Cause my old fridge ain't that good. I usually just use the window by my bed as my sort of fridge assist. Boy, I keep drinks cool there or even milk. An you know what it's really good for too? Makin' Jell-o. Real quick. Right there on the window sill. But anyways, I ask Bernie why he wants a new fridge. An would he be intrested in buyin' a really old Amana. "Nope. I'm gettin' a new one, Joe. The economy's on fire." "Really?" I says to him. That's funny. 'Cause the parts I'm stuck to mus be all wet or else everythin's burnin' aroun me and I'm just playin' the fiddle. If I had a fiddle. Or knew how to play one. The economy's on fire. "I can't even smell the smoke," I tell him. So he tells me about the economy an the budget surplus an everything. I gotta admit I got kine of bored but I was happy for him. An the government. Anyways, he asks me what I think they should do with the surplus. "Spend it, I guess," I tell him. "That's not too imaginative, Joe," Bernie tells me and he goes to buy a new fridge.

So I felt kine of embarrassed that I couldn't say something better than "Spend it, I guess." An then I remembered what we used to do with our old fridges we foun at the dump, come ski-doo time. Boy it's weird how that happens to us sometimes, eh? We're thinkin' one thing an then our brain thinks another. What's up with that? Anyways, we used to rip the doors off the old fridges an use them for sleighs. Boy, are they ever fast. Just like ice. An we'd ride around. An fall off. An ride around some more. Ahhh. Anyways, it got me thinkin', Hey, maybe we could find more new uses of old appliances. Like maybe usin' old stoves as house heaters. Boy, there's been more than once I had to open the oven and put it on to warm up the house. Boy, maybe we could even turn old dishwashers into little showers for pets. Except not have too many cycles on there. An rip the doors off too. I'm just improvisin' here. An the old microwaves could be something too. Except for sure not dryers for the pets, 'cause I've heard bad things happen if you try an dry stuff in your microwave. 'Specially little animals. Boy, you guys ever get scared there's gonna be a crack in yer microwave or else it'll go eeenh an then you open the door, but the microwave stays on and you'll get all flooded with radiation? That happens to me sometimes. What's up with that? But anyways, that's what I figure the government can do with their surplus. Just recycle it. They could open a store, like the army surplus there. 'Cept it'd be full of old money they didn't want no more. An you could come buy it. Like say, get five dollar bills for a toonie. Or whatever. Anyways, I'm just glad we're finely getting some back after all we've given. This is Joe from Winnipeg. Meegwetch.

The Stocks Markets an Outhouses

Hey you guys, this is me, Joe from Winnipeg. Today I'm gonna be talkin' to you about the stocks markets an outhouses. I gotta tell you a quick story, when I was small at Halloween we used to move the outhouse on my dad, eh. Just put it back a couple feet. So the hole was wide open. You do it at night so they can't see. But boy, the las time we ever did that was when my mom went outside instead of my dad. I never knew my mom knew so many swearwords. Anyways, boy, there's some weird stuff goin' on there, eh, with those stocks markets? What's up with that? It mus almost be Halloween. Even I was gettin' panicked. An I don't even got stocks in nothin'. I belonged to a credit union a long time ago, but I'm not sure if that counts. I keep meanin' to get my thirty-five cents out of that account, but I'd end up spendin' more on bus fare than's in that account. Anyways, I was gettin' scared too, eh? It got so bad I even had a nightmare. There I was on Bay Street in Toronto. Thinkin' why'd I put all my dough into mutual funds. I shoulda went for the ole standbys instead of the quick cash grab. Sell long an' buy shorts, I was tellin' myself. An now's the time to buy. 'Specially bonds. But this is just a correction, eh? I was tellin' myself. This ain't no crash. This ain't no eighty-seven. Or twenee-nine. I jus gotta get back in the game. An then I turned on my computer. An there was solitary, eh? Boy, my frien Marilyn works in an office an she showed me that solitary once there on her computer. She's real good at it. "How come you're not doin' work?" I asked her. An she says, that playin' helps relax her. "An besides," she says, "everybody plays it. There's people that's what they do most of the day is play solitary. An then when their boss comes, they hide it or else pretend like they're workin'." She plays Vegas style, three card draw. Real pro. Me I jus played one card draw. An I picked the cards that had the little haunted house an the bats 'cause it was Halloween. Who lives in that little castle I wonered. An why did they leave the lights on. An then I just woke up. Boy Joe, I tole myself, that's pretty scary. You dreamin' about livin' in Toronto. What's up with that? So I grab the paper to see if any of that stuff I was doin' in my dream I could really do. But that stocks market part of the paper I always just skip through. Kine of like the bad comics. I keep sayin' "Famly Circus." What's up with that? Who's reading it? But someone mus be. 'Cause they even went to the trouble of givin' the mommy a new haircut. But yet, P.J.'s still wearin' the same pyjamas. What's up with that? Me, I like "Dilbert." Anyways, now you're prob'ly thinkin', "Joe, what do you care about stocks for? You don't got none. You're not losin' money." But boy, let me tell you. Whenever stuff like that seems to happen it ends up affectin' me somehow. Maybe stuff ends up costin' more. Or jobs are harder to fine. Or whatever. I jus know it's like bein' the one who steps into that hole where the outhouse used to be. You don't see it comin' 'cause you thought everythin' was OK. But you gotta look. An be careful. Because somebody moved it. Boy, for those of you guys who got outhouses, make sure you take a big stick you tap the groun with in front of you. An you ladies who have men in yer lives, make sure that toilet seat's put down there, or you know what happens. Jus be aware. An make sure you give out lots of candy at Halloween. None of these toothbrushes an stuff. What's up with that? Me, I'm gonna try not to be too scared. Eat all the candy I give out when I hear that "Halloween Apples." Boy, I love that. This is Joe from Winnipeg. Meegwetch.

Assumpshions

Hey you guys, this is me, Joe from Winnipeg. Today I'm gonna be talkin' to you 'bout assumpshions. Boy, I'm glad to be back home. You know, I just got to tell you this one more thing about New York. I know, I know. You're thinkin', "Oh great, Joe went on a trip, so now he's gonna be talkin' about it all the time. Makin' us jealous and stuff." But I promise I won't do that. I don't want to be like these people who have vacations or operations and then they just keep talkin' about it. What's up with that? So, anyways, I was thinkin', you know what that New York City's really like? It's like a big wedding. 'Cause all you hear is horns honkin' all the time. Day an night. OK, I won't talk about that no more. So there's this thing about the new survey they did on Canadians, eh? An they foun that almost half of them would not become citizens if they all had to take a test. 'Parently, most of us don't even know the words to our own national anthem. What's up with that? "O Canada. Our home and native land." I doan have no problem 'memberin' that last line there, boy. It's a good reminder, I tell myself. An this survey's s'posed to be good nine times out of 10 with two percent margin of error or somethin' like that. I like how they always use math to say that their survey's good. Jus like the government. I guess they do that, so that maybe someone like me, Joe, doesn't go to the shopping mall and ask people stuff like if they know who Chief Dan George is? An if they don't I could say that Canadians don't know much about ''Nishnawbes either. I do think a survey might bear that out a little bit. But anyways, I was watchin' the Remembrance Day ceremonies and hearin' them sing "O Canada." And realizin', I don't know the words to "O Canada" too. They even got French in there now. I used to know the words, when that guy with the white hair would sing the anthems before the Montreal Canadiens played at the Forum. But you know, watchin' that Remembrance Day ceremony I saw all the stuff I take for granted. Like freedom. An TV. An this country. An that's dangerous, boy. Just two weeks ago, I went an applied for a job at this warehouse. Shippin' and receivin'. Although I doan know why they call it that, when really those guys are loadin' stuff. It's the truck drivers who're shippin' and receivin'. What's up with that? So anyways, I applied for this job. Did my interview and I was actin' all good 'cause I thought for sure I'd get it. I had my resume there with stuff like pumpin' gas, and sellin' ice cream. Even selling clothes. So I thought I was more than qualified. In fact, I even expected that job. It was an assumpshion. An when I found out I didn't get it, boy, I got mad. An then I was ashamed, eh. 'Cause nothin' should be assumed. We shouldn't assume that what those people in the war did for us was easy. An we shouldn't assume that we can jus live in this country without contributin' to it. We could at least learn our national anthem. An you know what? If some of us, me too, don't know what's goin' on in our own country, then that's dangerous too. So I'm encouragin' you here not to be assumpshionish. Be grateful for what you got 10 times out of 10. Every day. With no margin of error. An hey, let's not forget about some of our histry. Our prime ministers, like Tupper. An Mr. Borden. If his name wasn't on the hunerd dollar bill I wouldn't even 'member him at all. But then I don't see him too often. I'm more used to seein' the Queen and Laurier. An don't forget Kim Campbell. Or John Turner too. This is Joe from Winnipeg. Meegwetch.

Things Disappearin'

Hey you guys, this is me, Joe from Winnipeg. Today I'm gonna be talkin' to you about things disappearin'. I hate when people fight. 'Specially us Canadians. You guys hear who Parizeau's blamin' now? More ethnic people. What's up with this guy? "I'm just callin' a spade a spade," he says. Yeah well, my dad always used to tell me, "A skunk smells hisself first." I'll let you guys figure that out. But anyways, I gotta tell you guys. I love where I live. The people in this province are the best. Hey, maybe it's our fault the Quebec people said no. I sure hope so. Just the other day, I was goin' to cash this little cheque I got. I doan know why I say little, all my cheques are little. Anyways, it was about nine o'clock an I was wanting to cash my cheque really bad, eh? So I says to myself, "Joe, why doan you go to the Money Mart?" But then I'd be losing money on the deal, an if I waited just another hour I could go to the bank. OK, I says to myself, that's what I'm gonna do. Go to the bank. An you know, it got me thinkin'. Didn't banks used to be open earlier before? How come they're open at 10 o'clock now? What's up with that? They should be open before people go to work. Or at least be open eight hours. A lot of 'em are only open six. So I get to the bank I usually go to, but I guess the last time I was there was about two months ago. Anyways, I get there an the bank's closed. I mean closed like closed. Closed down. Out of business. Well not really, like a bank would go out of business. Those guys are makin' more money than that Bill Gates. You guys read the *Enquirer*? I do whenever I'm at my frien Bernice's. She always buys that, eh? An they had a story in there sayin' if Bill Gates stopped to pick up a hunerd dollar bill on the groun on his way to work, he'd lose money. I'm not sure what that means, 'cause I know the only way I'd be losin' money from a hunerd dollar bill on the ground was if it was mine. Or else I just left it there. An I'm sorry to say, I doan think that would ever happen.

So anyways, this bank was gone. I stuck my head on the glass to try an see inside, but there was nothin' there. Just empty, eh? An there was a sign there that said "Sorry. Please try our other convenient locations at blah blah blah." Convenient? What's up with that? I came to this one 'cause it was convenient an now it's closed. So anyways, I was gonna leave, but then my frien Bird showed up. Bird's her nickname, eh? I think her real name's Robin. Anyways, we say hi, an she asks me what I'm doin' an I tell her. "Oh," she says to me. "I think the banks jus want us to use bank machines now. No more bank tellers. They're kine of disappearing, eh?" she says to me. "Like my mitts." An she shows me these tiny little gloves she's wearing. You could just see her wrists, eh? "My kids took my mitts," she says. "An they left me these. Things have a way of disappearin' at my house. Like pictures in my photograph albums. An little change from my change purse. An food. Boy, food really disappears at my house." An she went on an on. Boy so many things had a way of disappearin' I had to start goin', "yup," "uh hunh," "oh yeah." You know how we go to pretend we're really listenin'? But really we're jus lookin' for a way out of this conversation. So when Bird took a breath, I said, "I gotta go cash this cheque, Bird. I'll come visit you for tea soon." "Doan bother," she says, "that disappeared too." Boy, I sure respect parents. They do lots. But you know, Bird got me thinkin'. There's lots of stuff that's had a way of disappearin' lately. The ozone. Trees. My money. Banks. Corner stores. That show, *King of Kensington*. Even some people's hope. An boy, that's the worst one to disappear. Sometimes it's hard to hold onto something we need so much. An all I can say to you if that's the case is to try. Try really, really hard. 'Cause even if hope disappoints you, you'll always have more later. It's kine of like kids. It keeps comin' back. I hope you guys have good days. An remember, if you know what you got before it's gone, maybe you can fine a way to keep it. This is Joe from Winnipeg. Meegwetch.

New Year's

Hey you guys, this is me, Joe from Winnipeg. Today I'm gonna be talkin' to you about New Year's. I hope you guys had a good Chrismas. I know I sure did. Boy, did I eat lots. Lots of turkey. But no chickens. I was too afraid, eh? I didn't want to get that chicken flu. What's up with that? Us bein' able to get sick from animals. But then maybe that's where chicken pox comes from too, eh? Boy, that's right. Maybe even measles. That might come from weasles. Somebody maybe just put that double o upside down an it became a "m." But anyways, I'm thinkin' 'bout New Year's now that Christmas is over. An lots of things come to my mine, boy. Like the time I was a little kid an I had to babysit for my uncle. Me an' my cousin. 'Cept when my uncle came home he had a bit too much party in him. So me an my cousin sat there waitin' for our fifty cents each for babysittin' all night. But neither one of us was brave enough to ask for the money, eh? So my uncle made soup. An then he made us watch him eat it. But you know what? I remember he passed out. An his ole head jus went right there in the soup. Like one of them birds with the hats you used to get an put on the side of a glass. An that's all it did was bob in an out of that red water. That's how my uncle's head went. Plop. Right in that soup. Boy, me an' my cousin was so fed up we left without gettin' our fifty cents. I guess we should've been worried that my uncle might've drownded. An that soup was chicken noodle too, eh? Boy, seems like those chickens are out to get us human beens. Must be revenge for all the chicken fingers an chicken noodles an chicken delights. Hey, you guys ever see that big chicken on the chicken delights? It's holdin' a plate of chicken. What's up with that? Like a chicken would feed us chicken. "Here you go. This is my famly. I cooked them up jus for you." OK, OK, I'll stop. But you know, the other thing New Year's makes me think of is all we been through in this pas year of 1997. Lots of bad things. Like people dyin'. An a bus crash. An that flood. But there was much good too. Like that flood. I'm not never gonna forget all the good I saw people doin' each other there. An I'm not never gonna forget that this was the year I got to know so many of my neighbours. It's funny how we can live so close to someone an' yet not even know them. What's up with that? But luckly we can change that, eh? Jus like the year's about to change. An we got to remember to put the right date on our cheques. Or on our papers in school. But you can rhyme it too to help you remember. Jus change the date it's ninety-eight. An finely. Last thing I'm gonna say about New Year's is the mos important part. The kisses. If you do got someone to kiss. Make sure it's a good one eh? One where that person goes, "ahhh." 'Cause that's gonna be your firs kiss of the year. You got to start it off right. An if you don't got someone to kiss. You will. If that's what you want. Or else kiss your teddy bear. Or else your arm. There's lots of ways to practise kissin', boy. Ole Joe learned how to kiss from the mirror. An if you kiss your relatives make sure you wipe your mouths first. Sloppy kisses are only good if it's not yer relative. An make sure if you party you do it responsibly. Don't en up kissin' soup like my ole uncle. An to all of yous I wish a Happy New Year with much love an lots of kisses. This is Joe from Winnipeg. Meegwetch.

Deals

Hey you guys, this is me, Joe from Winnipeg. Today I'm gonna be talkin' to you about deals. All kines of deals. So I decide I'm gonna dress up a little bit, eh? So I'm puttin' on my shirt an my pants and then I look and see I only got one pair of black socks, eh? I'm always losin' socks. What's up with that? Sometimes I only got one of the pair an sometimes I can't fine them at all. So anyways, I put on the only pair I got an then I see that there's a big hole in them there on the heel, eh? Boy, was I embarrassed, but at least my shoe would cover up that hole. So I get ready to go downtown to the New Music Festival eh, 'cause someone gaved me free tickets. An was the bus ever full. So I got a seat excep my legs were all scrunched up, eh? An I could feel the air on my skin through that hole in my sock 'cause I was almos on my toes there. I felt for sure like everybody was lookin' at that hole in my sock, eh? An I'm thinkin', that teaches me right for tryin' to get a deal on socks. I bought like 10 pair of them for eight bucks. An this was the last pair I had left. An jus then someone taps me on the shoulder. Boy, did I ever jump. An I turn aroun and there's my lawyer frien Harvey. I know to some of you that's an oxymoron, eh? lawyer frien. But I doan like calling Harvey a moron, eh? So we talk a bit an then I offer Harvey one of my free tickets. "Boy, thank you my frien," he says to me. "Thank you very much for your largesse." "What?" I says to him, 'cause I couldn't figure out why he's insultin' me. "Thanks for your largesse," he says to me. "It's not that big," I tell him. An then he explains what that *largesse* means. That Harvey's always tryin' to use big words, eh? An then he tells me he's agog. Imagine this guy thinkin' he's a god? What's up with that? I thought he wanted to be a lawyer, not a doctor. Anyways, we both go to that music festival, but I can't help thinkin' about deals, eh? Like that thing with Bill Clinton an that Monica. How come she's gotta make a deal to tell the truth. An I may not be the quickest waboosh in the forest, but I thought of something with that Bill Clinton thing. Someone's lying. That's all that matters. An then the real big deal here in Canada. Those two big banks that want to become one. Who is that good for? Sure not you an me. The only thing I know about stuff gettin' bigger is that it's the little ones that get hurt. Deals. Deals. Deals. Eh? Where's that Monty Hall when you need him. They should always get a Winnipegger when it comes to makin' deals. We're the bes. Like that thing with the President of the Nunited States. Here's the deal. Somebody tell the truth an in return you get respect. An we all get to watch somethin' interestin' on TV instead. An for the banks. Instead of tryin' to give us jus door number one. We keep things like they is an we get to pick door number one, two, an three, eh. Let's make a deal where nobody's gettin' ripped off. An you get 10 pairs of socks that last you for 10 months not 10 days. You know I always used to wanna be the guy in the audience at the en of that *Let's Make a Deal*, eh? Where Monty bought lightbulbs an matches an stuff for 50 bucks. Boy, I woulda took all the junk I had an gone there. I know that's kine of like rippin' Monty Hall off, but if he wants those things for so much money...hey. Wait a minute. Maybe that's what all this deal stuff is about. Maybe us human beins like makin' deals where we're gettin' the better of somebody, eh? Instead of findin' the better of ourselves. I hope you guys make good deals today. This is Joe from Winnipeg. Meegwetch.

'Lympics

Hey you guys, this is me, Joe from Winnipeg. Today I'm gonna be talkin' to you about the 'Lympics. Boy, ole Joe got sick. My voice has one of those frogs in it, eh? I caught a cole somewhere. An that's a strange expression. Caught a cold. What's up with that? We usually only say we caught somethin' if it's what we want. Like I caught the person of my dreams. Or I caught the bus jus in time. None of us want coles. So why do we say we caught them. They caught us. Anyways, I was at that Youth Career Sym pose ium the other day eh. 'Cause I heard they needed chairs. An I had a hole bunch of them from the wrestlin' training centre. That seems to be one good thing you need if you're gonna be a wrestler is how to use a foldin' up chair to hit someone over the head with. So I headed over to the convention centre with some dented up chairs, those wrestlers have hard heads, boy. An there was a hole bunch of young peoples there. An they even held the door open for me an my chairs. Meegwetch, I says to them. An I walk in there an register an they give me a name tag, eh. So I put that on my ches. Hello my name is Joe, it says. An I'm walkin' into one of those rooms an I hear someone sayin', "Joe?" Boy, I was scared at firs, 'cause I thought it was a bill collector or someone else I owed money to an they finely tracked me down. But I turn around an there was this beautiful young woman. An' she says, "Are you Joe from Winnipeg?" "Yeah," I says, "how'd you know?" An she says, "From your name tag. An I reconize your face from the radio." "Really?" I says to her, an she says, "Yeah, your face belongs on the radio." Boy, I was jus proud, eh? An then I figured that out what she was sayin' to me. So I foun out her name was Sarah Miller with an aitch an that she wanted to make her famly proud an get a good career. An I tole her maybe she could become a hockey player. 'Cause they make good money. An there's womens hockey in the 'Lympics now. An she said, "Nahh. I like my nose the way it is." Boy, she got a point there, eh. But those Olympics boy. They spen millions of dollars on them an then it's like the 'Cademy awards, we all forget about them after they're over. The only reason I 'member the '88 'Lympics is 'cause they were in Calgry. An before that the '76 'Lympics in Montreal. But I 'member those ones more 'cause we're still payin' for them. An they finely got that roof on there, but I doan think it works too good, eh? That's one thing 'bout roofs. If you need roof work you know yer gonna have to pay for it. But the other thing about that 'Lympics is that they make us proud of our countries, eh? An proud of the peoples that go there for us. Like all the speed skaters. An the womens hockey players. An the curlers. Especially the curlers, 'cause those guys are playin' what to me is pure sports. Throwing rocks. That should be a 'Lympic sport too. Rock throwing. Not the shotputs, but throwing rocks. For accuracy. An for skipping. An see who can hit power lines with rocks the bes. Boy, those lines jus go vooo when you hit them with rocks, eh. But anyways, the other thing about those 'Lympics is they're something that make us feel like Canadians. An make us proud. But I'll tell you something else that makes me proud. When I see young peoples tryin' hard. An when peoples hold doors open for each other. They should have 'Lympic medals for kineness. I think Winnipeg would do pretty good at those. This is Joe from Winnipeg. Meegwetch.

Roads

Hey you guys, this is me, Joe from Winnipeg. Today I'm gonna be talkin' to you about roads. I know what yer thinkin', "Oh yeah, Joe's gonna give us the metaphor about roads. Roads are this. Or roads are that." Forget it. I'm not gonna do that. OK. So my frien asked me to go canvassing with her for the kidney month. An at firs I said, what do you need me for? I'm jus gonna scare the people. 'Cause this was a kine of nice neighbourhood an' I didn't see many 'Nishnawbe people livin' aroun there eh. But she says to me that she needs me to help her in case there's dogs, 'cause she's real scared of dogs, eh? So I said, OK 'cause she appealed to the macho part of me an' I felt I needed a change of pace since I was at the Chiefs' conference they had at the convention centre. An I felt sorry for my leaders, 'cause they were arguin' about the same thing the res of Canada's arguin' about. Unity. What's up with that? Seems to me if you gotta argue about unity yer not very nunited. But anyways, me an my frien started the canvassing for the kidney foundation, eh. An I notice my frien was kine of anxious to do this, an' I thought maybe 'cause she had to ask for money, that's always hard, eh? Some of my friens do that all the time. An then I thought it mus be 'cause of the potential dogs that I was gonna protec her from, eh? But I kine of thought about that a bit, an the bes thing I could think of doin' to protec her if a dog attacked was offerin' my arm for the dog to chew or else my leg to bite instead of my frien's. Here was ole me tryin' to be macho an now I see what the mailpeople are always complainin' about. The street we were on was called Door Chester an why they name a street after some guy's door I doan know, but if Monty Hall gets a street too then that's OK with me. An boy, you know what? That street was jus full of potholes eh? Ahh, the springtime in Winnipeg. Lots of san. Brown. The smell of dog's business. An potholes. Boy, I gotta tell you I jus felt like I was back home on the reservation. That road on Door Chester was so bad my frien's shocks mus be shot by now. But I gotta say, we only ran into one dog an he was kine of old an confused 'cause he kept barkin' sideways at us, eh? Like as if we were standin' away from him. Or else maybe that was 'cause only one of his eyes worked good. I doan know. An the next house we went to the person that lived there was scared. I thought it was 'cause of me, but then I figured out that she wasn't used to visitors. But then I saw somethin' I never seen before, eh? We went to this one house an there was a cat there. An I joked oh oh, there's a watchcat. Boy, when I said that, that cat jus attacked me. I'm jus kidding. Me an my frien looked at that cat and it had six fingers. Or paw extensions. Or toes. Or whatever you call those things the cat's claws sit in. Boy, I never seen nothing like that before, eh? True story. I'm jus betting that cat's name is Anne Bowlin. Like that one of Henry eight's wife who had 6 fingers. I thought for a secon an extra finger might be nice, for scratchin' my back or else bein' more discreet with my nose, but then I figured I'd have to cut holes in my gloves or else hope I could fine irregulars with an extra finger sewn on there. Anyways, all the things I saw, Chiefs fightin' over unity, cats with six digits, rotten roads in nice neighbourhoods, old dogs that bark sideways, an people bein' generous to the kidney foundation made me glad. Glad that some people have nice houses. Glad that I doan got a house that would end up costin' me six digits. An the taxes to pay, when you en up with roads like on the reserve? What's up with that? An glad that I didn't have to let some wicked dog chew my leg. An glad that helpin' my frien volunteer felt good in my soul. 'Cause we gotta take care of that too, eh? Or else like that road you en up with a bunch of potholes. Oh. I guess thas a metaphor. An one las thing, talk to yer neighbour. They're prob'ly nice like you. This is Joe from Winnipeg. Meegwetch.

Yams

Hey you guys, this is me, Joe from Winnipeg. Today I'm gonna be talkin' to you 'bout yams. Not the kine you put on bread, but the potatoey kind. I met a guy from the Scandinavia an' that's how he said jam, eh? Yam. I woner how he'd say yam? Anyways, what's up with this nuclear testin' by India? Now the 'Nunited States is all mad 'cause of this. Indians aren't s'posed to be testin' bombs. They're peaceful people. Didn't Gandhi come from there? Indians aren't s'posed to be like this. I guess if anybody's gonna be testin' nuclear weapons, it'll be them. An how come they need to tes them anyways? OK. Push the button. Yup. That bomb works. It'll kill people. Thas good, 'cause we weren't sure, you know. So oh yeah, yams. OK. So I was hungry the other day. As usual. An I figured I'd make some pomme frites, eh? Which made me wonder what do French people call french fries? Our fries? Anyways, I wen to the store an I was buyin' my provisions, which really was a thing of oil an potatoes. But you know what? They was sold out. Sold out of potatoes. I said to the clerk, "Hey, what's up with this? You guys aren't s'posed to run out of potatoes. Thas like runnin' out of milk." An he says to me, "Oh thas OK. We're sole out of milk too. We jus got buttermilk lef." An what's up with that? Who wants butter in their milk? An who buys this stuff? So I was mad, eh? An then I look an see these lonely little yams. An I figure, those are potatoes. I'll buy these an cut 'em up. Make my yam frites, eh. So I ask the guy if these are potatoes. An he says, "Yes. 'Cause they're also called sweet potatoes." So OK. I get home. I cut up the yams. An they're orange inside, eh? Kine of sof. Not very potatoey. An I get the oil ready there. Careful though or else you get flames up to the ceilin'. An doan wear short sleeves or else those little bubbles that pop out burn your arms, eh? So after I'm done, I eat my yam fries an they're OK. They are sweet. An I didn't mine them really. So OK. "Who cares about yer yams, Joe?" Well, as useshwal, yams make me think. My frien Fred was tellin' me him an this guy John was talkin' about 'Nishnawbe here in Winnipeg. An Fred mentioned he's a frien, eh? An this guy says, "Oh yes, Joe. The Happy Indian." Boy, that made me mad. It made me mad 'cause here was this guy, sayin' that I'm a yam, all sweet an' stuff, but really I should be a potato. 'Cause if I'm the "Happy Indian" then evry other 'Nishnawbe mus be the "Angry Indians" or the "Sad Indians." Look. I know 'bout pain. Evrybody does. An I know 'bout injustice. An sadness. An anger. An sometimes I talk about that, eh? But I like tellin' stories. An I like makin' people laugh. An I like people. For so long Native people have had to fight against so many things. Sometimes even almos givin' up. People sayin' you guys are dis. Or you should do dat. Or here, let us teach you. Let us take care of you. But not really. An now I feel like I got to defen bein' happy. If thas what I am. But human bein's are always much more. Happy. Sad. Grouchy. Finnicky. Ticklish. You name it. So. Me. I hope I change. I hope I get more happy. An grow. An maybe I yam a yam. Like Popeye. You know, that Popeye was a smart guy. He jus says to himself, "So what if I talk funny. An my forearms is bigger than my biceps. I know who I am an thas dat." Good advice. I think the cartoons have been our self-help books before somebody invented those. I hope you guys are all REALLY happy today. So when people talk 'bout you then they can say, "Oh, so an so, The Happy Person." Souns good to me. This is Joe from Winnipeg. Meegwetch.

Old, New and Vice Versus

Hey you guys, this is me, Joe from Winnipeg. Today I'm gonna be talkin' to you 'bout old, new and vice versus. But firs, have you guys heard the great news. The banks is makin' good profits again. Yay. 'Cause you know it's only been like…I can't remember when they had a bad year. But you know what I was tinkin'. If the banks make their money out of our money, how come the government doesn't do that when they take our money? Ahh, but there I go, talkin' 'bout money. Who needs to hear that, eh? So old, new and vice versus. Well, I was goin' to see my frien Donna the other day eh, 'cause she got a new computer. Somebody gave it to her 'cause they tried to say it ruined their life somehow. Now what's up with that? Tellin' somebody that the thing you're givin' them can ruin their life. Turns out that person got addicted to the Internet, eh. They couldn't communicate properly unless they had a screen on there. Donna tole me her frien grunted something at her when she picked it up an their han was all twisted up from using that mouse ting. Anyways, before I wen over there I had to pick up a pen, 'cause they let you say stuff without 'lectricity. So I got my pen at the convenience store, an you know what? I saw a bank machine in there. An then I realize they're in all the convenience stores eh? The 7-Elevens are becomin' our new banks. Which is jus like the old days, 'cause thas where people used to get their supplies, an trade furs an stuff, was at the store. Kine of like a bank. An then I remember how that the RCM police is celebratin' their birthday. You know, I heard someone say they brought the law an order to the wes, 'cause I guess the 'Nishnawbe didn't have that before they got there. But I'm glad we still got them aroun, 'cept the Mustangs they ride now got eight cylinders, eh. An when I got to my frien Donna's there was two computer guys there eh, Len an Eric, they were fixin' somethin'. Or whatever. That poor little computer was jus like an operation, layin' on the table, with some guys pokin' aroun inside it. An then I thought, hey, these guys are the new doctors for the nineties, eh? Makin' house calls like doctors used to do in the old times. An now that old was new an vice versus. All this stuff we had from the ole time was new again, eh. I even see the Jewish people and the 'Nishnawbe workin' together again. I even heard once someone try tell me that the 'Nishnawbe are the los tribe of the Israel. An someone tole me the same ole story in a new way, vice versus, that the Jewish people are the Seafoam people an they come from the 'Nishnawbe. Boy, I doan know 'bout that, but I'm glad they're helpin' each other. 'Cause one thing our peoples have in common is a histry of suffrin'. But anyways, after Donna got her computer set up there, she says to me, "OK, Joe. There's my computer. Let's send the e-mail to somebody." "Like who?" I says to her. "I doan know," she says. So I sugges that we write the e-mail with my pen an then sen it to somebody, eh? So thas what we did. So if you get that e-mail on the piece of paper doan get mad 'cause it's not on a computer. It's jus a new way of doin' the ole ting of sayin' hello. This is Joe from Winnipeg. Meegwetch.

Improvisisin'

Hey you guys, I'm Joe from Winnipeg. Today I'm gonna be talkin' to you 'bout improvisisin'. I know der's prob'ly too many syllables on dat word already, but a few more won't hurt, eh. So the other day I made a big plan, eh. I was gonna go see a movie with my sister. Dat's right. Joe's got a sister. I got a big famly. Dat famly tree of mine's pretty top heavy, eh. But anyways, we was gonna go see a movie. An so all day I was lookin' forward to that eh. I even had my six fifty saved up. Did you guys know they dropped the price of the movies? I guess too many people saying, "Hey, what's up with this? Almost 10 bucks for a movie now. I can rent three of dem for dat." I tink dat's what people did too, eh. We got so many ways to distract ourselves now der's a price war goin' on. So I'm all gettin' ready to go meet my sister, so I call her an say, "Hey where'd you wanna meet for dis movie?" An she says, "I gotta cancel." "What? How come?" An then she tells me dis whole long story about how our brother lost his cat an how my other brother who was gonna babysit ended up havin' to go help him look for his cat. Boy I was startin' to hate little Hoover, eh. Das the cat. I know it ain't fair an it's misdirected anger, but I was even gettin' mad dat my brother named his cat after a vacuum cleaner. No woner he took off. He was prob'ly sick and tired of all the other cats with the cool names like Shadow an Fluffy makin' fun of him eh. So anyways, my sister says, "You wanna come visit me instead?" "OK," I said. Boy, I was just pouting, eh. You know, I tink guys are the bes at pouting. We learn it somewhere in grade two an we never forget it. So I go to visit my sister an turns out my brother foun his cat in the closet, eh. Good place for the vacuum. Anyways, by dis time it was too late for the movie, so we went for a walk instead, eh. An we walked an talked, an I thought. Dis ain't too bad. It's not costin' us no money. An then we heard dis music, eh. Comin' from the exchange distric.

So we go over der an der's all dese people listenin' to jazz music, eh. Boy, was dat ever good. I like dat jazz music an I didn't even know it. An den my sister tells me she likes it too. An dat a part of jazz music is dat they improvize eh. Boy, den I realized right der: Dat's what our lives is, eh. Improvisisin'. We make plans an we try to follow dem, an sometimes dey work an sometimes dey don't. An sometimes life throws stuff at you dat you doan expec an you got to improvize, eh. So I asked my sister how she knew all dis stuff about the jazz music an she read it in the paper. Boy, I asked her some more questions like did you plan to bring us to dis jazz festival? An she jus laughed, eh. It didn't matter though. 'Cause I had a good time makin' it up as I go. An thas what's great about bein' a human been, we can make stuff up, figure tings out as we go along. An der's nothin' wrong with that. You know, some of us try an figure everythin' out, have everythin' planned. Controlled. An sometimes you need dat, eh. But mose of the time we're flyin' by the seat of our pantses. I know I am, an I doan even know how to fly. In fac, I'll prob'ly be improvisisin' for the res of my life. If only I could cook like dat, eh. I'm Joe from Winnipeg. Meegwetch.

Kids

Hey you guys, this is me, Joe from Winnipeg. Today I'm gonna be talkin' to you about kids. Not the kine dat are billy goats, but the kine we see all aroun us. Come in all shapes an sizes an colours an even volume settings eh. 'Cept it's like a broken stereo. You can't turn it up or down, it's jus stuck on the 10 or the two. Whatever. Anyways, I been wanting to talk about kids for a long time, eh. So now I'm finely doin' it. I had an amazing ting happen to me too, eh. But I'll get to dat later. So my frien went to a baby shower the other day, eh? I doan know why it takes 10 people to shower a little baby, must be a real dirty little kid. Just kidding. Anyways, der was dis woman der an she had her new little baby, cute little girl, eh. I didn't ask my frien for her name, but dis little baby's the fluffy kine, with the little rolls on the arm an the cute little cheeks dat you jus wanna pinch. Anyways, some peoples have been tellin' her dat her little baby girl should lose weight. What's up with that? It's a baby. The fatter the better I say. It makes me mad dat some of us is tryin' to impose unrealistic body images on little girls before they even know how to work their body. Or dat they even have one. An if someone's overweight 'cause they can't help it. Leave 'em alone. Sorry. I'm gettin' carried away eh. I got a new attitude towards kids now. I always loved 'em, but now I wanna protec 'em too, eh. So, my amazing moment. The other day, I was on the bus, comin' back from the reserve. An I went to use the facility in the back of the bus. So I walk to the back tryin' not to fall over, 'cause dis bus was shakin' from side to side. Anyways, I get der an I look at the door an the little ting says, Unoccupied, so I open the door. An standing der with his back to me is a little boy using the bathroom. He looks at me an I shut the door real fas an say sorry. Dis all happened in about one secon eh, but it kine of slowed down for me. 'Cause in dat one instant when I opened dat door an saw dat little boy, I realized Ho boy, we gotta protec our little ones. Little kids are so vulnerable, eh. They don't know tings. They get in trouble. They make mistakes. An we should forgive children all tings, eh. 'Cause dey're children. We sometimes go forgetting dat. An protecting kids is all of our responsibility even if dey're not our own kids. I wish I could share with yous how dat felt on dat bus. Jus 'cause dat little guy didn't know how to lock the door on the toilet he got walked in on. An der's lots of other ways kids doan know they can be in trouble too, eh. Now I'm not saying dis stuff to make people paranoid, eh. We can all do a good enough job of dat ourselves, but jus remember dat children are like little eggs. An we're the box. We gotta hold them an keep them safe, 'cause dey're the biggest reason for us bein' here. I'm Joe from Winnipeg. Meegwetch.

Summer Fish

Hey you guys, this is me, Joe from Winnipeg. Today I'm gonna be talkin' to you 'bout summer fish. I'll explain dat in a minute. So dis ting goin' on with the Tories. What's up with that? What a mess, eh? You'd tink dey could fine a leader who got people excited. Like the underwear guy, Stanfield did in the sixties. An the other Tories here in Manitoba. Now what's down with that, eh? Some people sayin' they used 'Nishnawbe candidates to split the left. I doan know if dat's true or not, but I'll tell you someting, the left doan need the Tories' help splitting. Dey'll do dat demselves tank you very much. I'm jus kine of glad they consider us 'Nishnawbe as votin' for the left. But we're people, eh, so a lot of us prob'ly vote for the right too. So anyways, dat's not quite a minute, but I said I was gonna talk about summer fish. Now the fishermen here know what I'm talkin' about, but der's a diffrence between summer fish an winter fish. Know what it is? Da taste. Personally, I tink the summer fishes taste better, eh. Dat's 'cause dey're stronger. Rather dan havin' a subtle, delicate flavour dat teases the palate with the promise of more, dey're strong, eh. Dey taste wilder. Ting is, I doan know why dey're like that, I tink it has to do with what they eat. Now yer prob'ly wondrin', "Joe, why are you talkin' 'bout fishes an how dey taste an da summer an winter an delicate flavours?" Well, it's 'cause summer fishes is one of my favrit tings of the season here in Manitoba. An seasons too. Not ev'ry place gets dem, you know. Dey jus get the borin' constant warm teperature like in Florida. What do those guys do at Christmas? Santa Claus wouldn't have no sleigh. No snowballs. Snowmobiles. Or even weather forecasters, eh. "An how's da weather lookin' today?" "Well, it's gonna be nice an mild. Again." An all der fish would taste the same. We're very lucky here in the middle of Turtle Island, eh. 'Cause we need tings to compare so we know what we got. Like seasons. Cars an trucks. Cats an dogs.

Governments. Even people too, eh. So I hope you guys have a good summer. 'Cause dat's one ting we know how to enjoy here is da summers. Me, I'm gonna eat lots. 'Specially summer fishes. An I'm gonna sleep. Two tings I'm good at. Bet you didn't know some of us are better at sleepin' dan others, eh. It's true. Der's lots of us who are better unconscious dan conscious. An some of us you can't tell what dey are. I hope you guys have a good time dis summer. I'll miss yous. Absence makes the heart grow fonder. If dat was true my teacher would've been more understanding of my absences. But anyways, I'll tink of yous an pray dat yer makin' the mose of whatever yer doin'. Have a real good summer. I'm Joe from Winnipeg. Meegwetch.

Food Faces

Hey you guys, this is me, Joe from Winnipeg. Today I'm gonna be talkin' to you about food faces. What the heck is that, Joe, you're wondrin'. Well just wait a minute and I'll tell you. So anyways, I was sittin' down to watch the news and I'm feeling kind of hungry, eh? And you know there used to be a time when I had to learn how to ignore that hunger, but now since I got my own bachelor pad I tell myself, Joe, live high on the pig. You deserve that to yourself. So I get up and walk across the room to my cupboard and I'm telling myself, Joe, I says to myself, make sure it's something low fat and no additives or preservatives. I should just have some water, I answer myself. It's funny how we can talk better to ourselves than other people, eh? What's up with that? Anyways, I get to my cupboard and boy, did I ever feel like that old goose. My cupboard was bare. Well OK, that's eggsagerating I did have a bag of Quaker oats. The quick kind. Come to think of it, I've never had the slow kind. They should be offerin' that to us consumers. What's up with that? Anyways, I look at that smiling white guy with the white hair and the big kind of cowboy hat and son of a gun if that guy ain't got a bib on already. So I pick up the bag and read it. Low fat. That's good. Source of dietary fibre. That's good too. Hunerd percent whole grain. No additives or preservatives. I start thinkin' no wonder this stuff needs lots of brown sugar. But you know what? I had no Quaker oats left. I'm kind of mad at first, but then I figure, just go get some more. And I look on that bag and I see it says, "It's the right thing to do." Trademark. I guess I gotta do somethin' now for sayin' that. Anyhow, I take that as a message and head off to the new SuperValu. Boy that place is big, and I tell myself: No impulse buying today, Joe. Just get the oats and get out. So I go to the cereal section to find the guy with the white hair and the big kind of cowboy hat and I pass by the rice and even something called Red

River Cereal. I never knew I tell myself. You know a region must be important if its got it's own cereal. And then I get to the pancakes. That's temptin', I tell myself and then I did that with my head. Oh, I guess you can't see that, but if you picture me twisting my head to the side twice, that's what I did. And I look at the pancakes mixes and there's Aunt Jemima. Smilin' away, with that one pearl earring and a lace collar. 'Cept she looks diffrent. And I look closer and I hit my head with the bottom of my hand. Holy smoke, I says, where's her kerchif? They took away Aunt Jemima's kerchif. What's up with that? I tell myself and then I stop. And head voice says, you KNOW, Joe. You know why she's not got that kerchif on her head no more. And I pick up that box and look closer at her, twist it around a bit and there I see that white-haired guy. He's on the box too. Same company. And I look up and I see cream of wheat and there's another person of colour on that box. Smiling. Just like Aunt Jemima. 'Cept he's still got his head covered with a chef toque. I know it's not a toque, but that's what it reminds me of. Boy and I remember the rice back up that aisle, and I look and there's Uncle Ben. All these food faces lookin' at me. Smiling. And right away I grab a bag of wild rice to see if there's an Indian guy on there. Smiling or something. But there wasn't. And I felt relief. And then I remember, hey what about that Betty Crocker, isn't she some kind of computer-generated ethnic mix or something? Not even real. Was Aunt Jemima someone real? How 'bout the creamed wheat guy? Or Uncle Ben? Whose uncle was he? Is he s'posed to be my uncle? Your uncle? And how does a person of colour feel when they look at these foods? I bet it's not relieved. And then I ask myself a question. Using people of colour as food faces. Is this the right thing to do? And I answer myself before I even finish the question. Boy, that's neat how our brains can do that. If it was the right thing to do, how come Aunt Jemima doesn't got a kerchif no more? What's up with that? I ask you. Me, I bought no name oats and went home. This is Joe from Winnipeg. Meegwetch.

Mouses

Hey you guys, this is me, Joe from Winnipeg. Today I'm gonna be talkin' to you 'bout mouses. I almos said "meeses" eh, like Jinx the Cat. He hates the meeses to pieces. Boy, me too. Sort of. So anyways, boy, it's good to get my big mouth back on the radio here. I missed talkin' to you guys. I was drivin' my fam'ly crazy. Always commentatin' on stuff. Hey, how 'bout dat Clinton and Monica. What's up with that? I'd say. An how 'bout the stocks markets? What's up with that? An the Russian thing? What's…you get the idea. Boy, dey did too, eh? Tellin' me to go bug somebody else. So here I am. Anyways, mouses. So I was watchin' the wind move the trees the other day eh. Sittin' der eatin' a choclate bar. An den I hear dis funny noise. "Chick a chick a chick a chick." Boy, I looked at my bar to see if I was eatin' the wrappin' again, eh. But I wasn't. So I sat der an watched a little more. Da leaves were makin' that soun, like, "See ya. Be back nex year." I know some of yous is wondrin' why I'm watchin' the win, eh? I figured it was time I do more Native type stuff. So anyways, den I hear this "chick a chick a chick a chick" soun again eh. Boy, dis time I wait. An den I listen to hear where dat "chick a chick a chick" comin' from. An I look, an I see dis other choclate bar I dropped on the floor from before eh. Boy. An der was a mouse eatin' it. I jumped up from my chair 'cause I was so shock, eh. Boy, den I wen into cat mode right away. I crouch behine my chair an I watched that choclate. Den I get dis funny feelin' eh. An I turn my head an look by the rad e ator an der's dis little grey head peekin' out an lookin' at me. Boy, I jumped again. An dat mouse took off. But in dat momen our eyes met. I knew it was war, eh. So I wen an grabbed a shoe. An I sat by the door waitin' for him, 'cause dat was his only escape. An after sittin' der for about two hours an tinkin' bad tings like, Who do I know's got a gun, eh? I wen to go ask my frien Laughin' Louie. Dey call him dat 'cause he laughs all the time, eh. Myself, I can tink of a better nickname to have. So I ask Louie, "How do I get rid of dis mouse in da house, eh?" An he says to me, "You got a hammer?" An I says, "Yeah." An he says, "Can I borrow it?" "What for?" I says to him. "So I can nail someting," he says to me an den he laughs. An den he tells me to jus put out traps. So I did. An I even used dat choclate he was eatin'. Sure enough nex morning dat choclate was gone an dose traps was unset, eh. So den I heard, put peanut butter on der. So I tried dat. An I could swear, eh, dat dat little mouse lef me a note wanting some jam too. Boy, by dis time I was so frustrated. An den I figured it out about dis little mouse. He's jus like us, eh. Tryin' to make a livin'. Tryin' to get by. I even figured dat I didn't really wanna kill him. Dat was jus me tryin' to be macho. Or do what I always heard you're s'posed to do. Da best ting would be to trap him an throw him in a field somewhere, eh. Or else give him a 'viction notice. Dis one's so smart I bet he can read. So I'm gonna leave him alone for now. He's been doin' dat for me. He's even been doin' his busness where I can't see it, eh. So I guess dat's what I'm sayin' to yous, is dat when yer tryin' to get by today, do yer bes to avoid the dummies like me, holdin' der shoes over der head. An dat even dey aren't all bad. Sometimes we all get a little obsessed, eh. Look at dat old Ken Starr. What's up with that? If him an me was after dat mouse we would've blowed up the house by now. This is Joe from Winnipeg. Meegwetch.

NSF

Hey you guys, this is me, Joe from Winnipeg. Today I'm gonna be talkin' to you 'bout the NSF. Or maybe I should jus say NSF, if I say "the" NSF then you might tink I'm talkin' 'bout an organization der. An what's up with dat anyways, eh? How come we got to make the names of stuff into letters? Like the NHL. Or the AMC. CFS. IBM. CBC. Does dat mean we're lazy? Or is it kine of like a nickname? I doan know. Maybe it's to make it soun more intimidatin', eh. I know if I'm dealin' with a place known by its letters it's either really big or else it can do scary tings. Like the CSIS, eh? I doan even know what dat las one stans for it's so secret. So anyways, NSF. I got a bill back 'cause the cheque I wrote had the NSF, eh. Not sufficient funs. I was waitin' for like a refun from the goverment. Well actually it was my frien's cheque, but I always like to be the one who has the good news an han dem der cheque like they jus won the lottery, eh. I tink dat would be a good job too. Hanin' out the lottery cheques to da winners. 'Cept I tink you'd get jealous after a while. Pretty soon you'd be, "How come dey get to be millionaires an not me?" Boy, dat's crazy. Anyways, instead of my frien's cheque, I get a bill. An the bill tells me my cheque was no good. The NSF eh. So dey was informin' me dat dey wanted der money an dat dey were chargin' me for da bad cheque. An da bank was chargin' me for da bad cheque too, eh. Boy, I jus felt like a criminal. Mad at myself. An mad at dese guys for chargin' me for my mistake. I didn't write dat cheque bad on purpose, eh. Boy did I feel stupid, eh. An embarass. An how come dey get to charge us for da mistake? What's up with that? How come we doan get to charge dem money if dey make a mistake or fail to provide a service, eh? We could jus walk in da bank der an say it's the kine of bank where der open but der's no teller service, an we could say, "Hey. You guys owe me 20 bucks. Plus I wan dis cheque cashed." Oh well, I guess it serves me right for not bein' more fiscally responsible, eh. I should use our governments as da example. Dey never write bad cheques. So after I tole my frien da bad news dat der cheque didn't arrive, she said, "Oh dat's OK. You know what happened to me?" "No," I says. An den she tells me the story of how a 'Nishnawbe on da street asked her for money 'cause he was NSF in his life, eh. An she gave him some. An he said, "Tank you." An she said, "Meegwetch." An I guess dis guy never heard somebody who wasn't 'Nishnawbe talkin' his own language to him before, eh. An she said his eyes lit up an she even taught he was gonna give her back da money he was so happy. Dat's a funny ting what can happen when we say what we mean in a way we unerstan, eh? Maybe we call tings by letters like say, CFS or NSF 'cause we're not too happy with what dey are eh? Sometimes I wish da places dat sent us money was more like our relatives. Instead of NSF dey could put a note in der, "Hey. Where's our money? An don't sen cheques. Cash or money order only." But den if dey was more like my famly I guess I'd take my time to pay dem back more. I keep gettin' surprised dat whenever I get in a bad mood 'cause of money or not havin' sufficien funs I get taught da same lesson over an over again. It's not dat importan, eh. Money comes an goes, but stuff like the 'Nishnawbe guy on the street, you never forget dat. I can't remember none of all da money I've had. I'm Joe from Winnipeg. Meegwetch.

Moose on the Road

Hey you guys, this is me, Joe from Winnipeg. Today I'm gonna be talkin' to you 'bout moose on the road. I had dat dessert all prepared too eh and den I went an dropped it. "Oh no," I says out loud, "my mousse is on da road." Jus kiddin'. Das not da kine of mooses I mean. You know one ting I love about talkin' words out loud? You doan have to be too literate, eh? Moose souns the same if it's da dessert or da animal or even da guy in da Archie comics. Moose. I tink da politicians like dat too eh? 'Cause den if dey say someting like say, "I need more time," an we say we waited long enough already, then they could say, "I'm talkin' bout the spices der." Or no could become k-no with a double o on der. Jus never stops, eh. Even when day say, "I doan lie." Dey could mean dey sleep standin' up. It's a good ting promise means da same no matter how you say it. Anyways, boy I missed you guys. I fell asleep on the bus an ended up in Thompson, eh. I woked up an I looked aroun an I said, "Where is dis beautiful place?" An den I saw some of dose Thompson turkeys, eh. Big black birds. I'm not sure why dey're called turkeys, maybe 'cause dat's da Tanksgivin' bird up der. I doan know. So anyways, I figured I came dis far why doan I go a little bit further. So I did. An den I ended up in Gillam. More beauty up der too. I even foun a shirt der with my name on it. So I put dat on. An den I went even further up north to Tadoule Lake. Wow. Das all I could say, eh. 'Cause it was beautiful an dey still have der language an culture. I was jus jealous. An den I was all ready to go on further adventures up in da north eh, even past da North of 60, but I figured I should come home. So I did. I ended up drivin' for my new frien Conway. I got to drive an he got to sleep. What's up with dat, eh? How come da passengers always get to sleep, not the driver? Anyways, I was tinkin'. Man, dis place we live in is BIG. Really big. An den I saw someone walkin' on da road. Way far away. An I got all excited 'cause I was gonna pick dem up. Even if dey weren't hitchhikin', I was gonna make dem a hitchhiker. An dat road from Gillam is hilly eh. Imagine dat. Hills in Manitoba. I get so prairie-centric sometimes, eh. Anyways, as I get closer I see dat dis person on da road turns sideways an has four legs. In my head I was sayin, "Is dat what I tink it is?" An my passenger said it out loud, eh. Dat kine of scared me for a minute 'cause dat's all he said on da whole trip. An sure enough. Der it was. A moose on da road. I wasn't even disappointed dat I wouldn't have a hitchhiker now, eh. I was jus happy to see dat ole moose. So I drove all da way home. All fourteen hours, eh. Dat ole Conway jus kep sleepin'. I kep havin' to stick my head out da window to stay awake for a bit. You guys doan do dat, eh. Drive sleepy. I'm not doin' dat never again. Anyways, I get home an I go for a hamburger. I hate to say it but dat moose made me hungry, eh. I tink when some peoples who aren't 'Nishnawbe see a moose dey tink, "Ahhh Canada. I love dis country." Me, I look at mooses an tink, "Mmmm, supper." So anyways, I order dis burger an talk to my frien John an Roger an dis guy's starin' at me. An he says, "Are you Joe?" "Yeah," I says to him. An I was scared, eh? 'Cause dis guy was big. An he had a beard. An I asked him how he knew my name an he said. "It's on yer shirt." "Oh" I says to him. An den he shakes my han an says, "I'm Thor." Boy, I got scared again, eh. Den I see dat Thor's like the moose. He's not what I'm tinkin' he is. An den we talk an he even says "Meegwetch" to me. An boy, dat warmed my heart. Someone who ain't 'Nishnawbe usin' dat language. So doan be like me an tink a person's a moose when really dey're somebody nice. I'm Joe from Winnipeg. Meegwetch.

Peekaboo

Hey you guys, this is me, Joe from Winnipeg. Today I'm gonna be talkin' to you 'bout peekaboo. Is dat one word or not? Boy I doan know. Maybe if you have to spell dat word today you better put some hyphen in der jus to be safe. Otherwise you might en up with peoples correctin' yer spellin' for you. Das a funny ting about dat, eh. I'm not sure how to react. Like are you s'posed to say tank you when someone tells you you spelt say da word "ere" wrong. Like it's sposed to be E R R, not E R E. Maybe you could say, "To err is human." Even dough I tink dat should be said da way it souns eh, "errrr." Among da 'Nishnawbe whenever you make dat soun, "errr," it means like, "ever sick," or "dat's crazy." Anyways, 'nough 'bout spellin'. Back to da peekaboos. So I was playin' dat game eh. Peekaboo. Wit one of my little nephews. I love dat game 'cause it doan cos nothin', eh. An you can use whatever you got handy. Like a newspaper. Or da corner of da couch. Or even yer hans. So der we was, me an my nephew. Playin' peekaboo. An I would be jumpin' aroun tryin' to hide from him, eh. An den I'd jump out an say "surprise." Den my nephew says to me, "Uncle. Yer s'posed to say peekaboo. Not "surprise." An what does dat mean anyways peek a boo. What's up with that?" Boy, I was jus jarred, eh. I didn't even know what to say. So den I did dat ting dat adults an da governments do all the time eh. I tried an make what I just said make sense. "Oh uhh, I said 'surprise' because I knew you wouldn't like me to say peekaboo." But really I jus forgot to say peekaboo, I was jus too embarrass to admit I screwed up, eh. Den my nephew says, "Les not play dis anymore. Let's do da crossword puzzle instead." Boy, dey grow up so fas, eh. Here he is wantin' to do da crossword an he's only in grade eight. Oh well. But den sometin' else happened, eh. I got a call dat my brother was in da hospital. So I rush right over der, eh. An after I see dat my brother's gonna be OK we had to get him dressed, eh. He was sore an evrything, so he needed help. Boy, all you guys who help people get dressed. Dat's a good ting yer doin'. Dey appreciate it, eh. An I appreciate it now too. It's not easy. Anyways, I was helpin' him pull his shirt over his head der, eh. An when his head popped out I jus went, peekaboo. Boy, dat was dangerous, eh. If he hadn't been so sore he might've hit me, eh. Da look on his face. "Doan make me laugh," he says to me. "It hurts." Boy, dat's a funny ting, eh. Dat laughin' can hurt. Strange dat. But den dat's what dis peekaboo makes me tink too, eh. Our lives is so fragile, eh. An our bodies. We should have little stamps on us der dat say dat, "fragile." Sos we can remember to take care of ourselves, eh. 'Cause boy, one minute you could be playin' peekaboo wit yer nephew an da next yer helpin' somebody put on der underwears. I guess we gotta 'member life does a peekaboo on us all da time, eh. Sometimes good. Sometimes bad. We jus gotta make sure we keep on keepin' on. An if you need help, ask somebody, eh. Der's all dese good people out der who help other people without even askin' evry day. An if one of yous figures out what dat peekaboo means, let me an my nephew know, eh. We wanna make a crossword puzzle for dat. 'Cep I doan know what da clue might be. Eight-letter word dat's not surprise. This is Joe from Winnipeg. Meegwetch.

Great Expectations

Hey you guys, this is me, Joe from Winnipeg. Today I'm gonna be talkin' to you 'bout great expectations. Les examine dat work a little bit. Now I tink dat in dat novel Dickens, bein' the master storyteller dat he was, was intrested in examinin' da human condition. You guys knew I was kiddin', right? Dat's not da kine of great expectations I mean. But der is a tip der for you who have to explain or give yer 'pinion 'bout somethin'. Jus say it's got to do with da human condition. When I went to school I used to put dat for my answer all da time. Da teacher der would ask me, "Joe. What did Shakespeare mean when he wrote da *Hamlet*." "Human condition." I'd say. An den my teacher would jus smile an say, "dat is correc." Boy, dat's a good catch-all answer so's dat you look smart, eh. But be careful to change da subjec right away or else you might get caught. Like say someone says, "So, what do you think about da economic situation right now?" An den you say, "Oh. It's da human condition all over again, eh." An den dey'll nod an agree wit you. Den you say sometin' like, "Hey, what's up with dis weather eh?" An hey. What is up with dis weather? Das really what I'm talkin' 'bout today, eh. Da great expectation. As in da winter. Where is it? I got to tell you guys I'm gettin' freaked out. Las night I was throwin' out da garbage an I jus about got runned over by four peoples on bikes. Bikes yet. What's up with that? It's the en of November already an dese guys are ridin' bikes. An why not, eh? I guess dat's alright. It jus all seems kine of unnatural to me dough. Kine of like dat new haircut Preston Manning got, eh. I know dat's ole news, but I can't get dat ole picture of him out of my head. I guess I kine of expected him to look da same all da time, eh. Like my dad. He's had da same haircut for about fifty years. So I'm kine of use to his head lookin' a certain way. But I got to tell you one other strange ting, eh. I was goin' to da store da other day. An boy are der ever lots of shoppers out der. Anyways, I go to dat store an when I was goin' in, da door didn't open, eh. So I just stood der for a little bit. An den I realized what I was doin'. "Joe," I says to myself, "What are you doin'? Are you expectin' dat door to open by itself for you or something?" Boy, you know what? I was, eh. I'm so used to da automatic doors now dat I was expectin' dat one to jus open up for me without me doin' anything. An dat's kine of a scary ting, eh. I guess all expectations are. Whether dey're great or small. We may be expectin' dem to turn out good, or we may be expectin' dem to turn out bad, but it's dat waitin' an expectin' dat's scary. So. I guess what I'm sayin' is, whatever great expectation you have for today I hope you fine it. An you know what, I was thinkin' no matter how bad we expect a day to turn out der's always somethin' good in der, eh. Even if it's jus goin' home. Or even goin' to bed. I hope yer great expectation is realized today. An remember dat da winter is comin', eh. This is Joe from Winnipeg. Meegwetch.

Christmas

Hey you guys, this is me, Joe from Winnipeg. Today I'm gonna be talkin' to you 'bout Christmas. I just found out a strange thing the other day. I celebrate my favrit holiday tonight. Like the French people. At midnight, eh. Dat's when Joe an his famly opens der presents. We tried to open presents on Christmas morning like I foun out most people do, 'cept we all slept in, eh. So we figured we'd go back to da way it was. I foun this out from my frien Tom, eh. We were talkin' about the holidays an this opening the presents on Christmas Eve thing came out, eh. We was both shocked with each other, eh. I heard da rumours 'bout openin' yer presents on da Christmas day, but I never seen it, eh. An he heard rumours of da midnight Christmas eve celebrations too, but he never seen it, eh. It's good when you fine out about a new tradition. I just assumed most people did the midnight thing too, eh. Instead of jus some of us 'Nishnawbe an the French. I guess we can see da birth of the Metis people in dat common Christmas celebration. Although I guess da 'Nishnawbe didn't have Christmas like we do now. But da idea of love an respect we get with dis season was ushely around, eh. Boy, listen to me, just babbling on, eh. Get to the point, Joe. I will. I will. But first. What's up with this Christmas, eh? It feels like a good one. Is dat just me? Or is it evrybody? I hope so. 'Cause I want you guys to feel good things as the 1998 ends, eh. Tink of the year as a real big meal. An we're jus gettin' to the dessert part right now. Whatever your favrit dessert might be. Pumpkin pie maybe. Or else choclate ice cream. Maybe even da Christmas pudding, eh. So. The point. Oh yeah. Christmas. It's been hard for me to focus lately, eh. If you were tryin' to fix something on yer car an I was the guy holdin' the flashlight you'd be pretty mad at me right now, eh. I'd prob'ly be hummin', lookin' aroun. Wondrin' if der's dose little fuzzy tings in my belly button, eh. Tinkin' how I'll save removin' dose for later, eh. I feel sorry for you guys with da outies, eh? You don't get to do dat, but den maybe yer more hygenic or someting. I've been unfocused for a simple reason, eh. I feel good. I know there's always bad stuff goin' on in da world. An I'm not sayin' to ignore it all da time. But you got to take a break sometimes too, eh. Jus fine one minute. One measly little minute in da day to reflect. Think of something funny. Or happy. Or stupid. If you have trouble with dat last one, jus tink of me eh. Dat should help. I suggest dis, 'cause doin' dis is what made me feel good. I was runnin' aroun tryin' to do all da tings I forgot dis Christmas. Presents. Cards. Whatever. An I even missed my bus. So. I had to take a forced time out, eh. All dis happened when it was snowing der da other night. An I was waitin' in da bus shelter for da next bus, wishin' I could sit down without gettin' a cold bum. What's up with those metal seats, eh? Cold in the winter. Hot in the summer. Anyways, I started starin' ahead, eh. At nothin' in paticular. An I see dis couple, eh. Draggin' home a Christmas tree. 'Cept I tink dey was arguin' about which way to drag it, eh. Top first. Or bottom first. It looked like a male female kine of argument. But den dey hugged an dragged da tree sideways, eh. Boy. Dat made me tink. Right der is something more powerful dan love, eh. Forgiveness. An dat's what Christmas is to me. Forgivin'. Forgivin' life if it's been rough to you. Forgivin' yer loved ones. Even yer hated ones too eh. To shop is human, eh. To forgive. Dat's Christmas. Merry Christmas, my friends. This is Joe from Winnipeg. Meegwetch.

3D's

Hey you guys, this is me, Joe from Winnipeg. Today I'm gonna be talkin' to you 'bout 3D's. Did you guys see the hockey game on the TV last night? Boy, that was great. Even though we lost. It was still good seein' the hockey night in Winnipeg again. No disrespec to the Moose. But I did always wonder why they named themselves after big slow animals that are good to eat. What's up with that, eh? If you name a sports team after an animal it should instill the fear in the opponent, eh. Like say the Mighty Ducks. If they was just called the Ducks people would laugh at them. But you put mighty in der an boy you're talkin' scary. Maybe we could have the Mighty Moose. Maybe not. All I know is, I keep hearin' people sayin', "What's wrong with the professional sports? What's wrong with the hockey?" Look at what was goin' on here in Manitoba, eh. Looks kine of right to me. So anyways, 3D's. Well I kine of misled you der. Sorry. Since the 3D is s'posed to be so excitin' I thought I'd use dat. I've been hearin' how they got the 3D pictures. An 3D sound. So that these 'lectronic experiences are more real. What's wrong with real? Reality's a nice place to 'scape from, eh, but I still wanna live der. So the 3D I'm talkin' 'bout is really jus one "d" 3 times. It's decisions, eh. Decisions. Decisions. Decisions. I was talkin' with my frien da other day. She had so many decisions she had to make in her life that one day. With one big decision piled on da top. Boy, she was just askin' me for help, eh. "Joe. What should I do?" she said. "I doan know," I tole her. "Sometimes coffee's good black. Sometimes good with sugar. Sometimes milk. Sometimes both. I doan know." "Thanks" she says to me. "Yer lots of help." An I said, "Meegwetch." But den I kine of got in a little bit trouble for not reconizin' her sarcastic tone, eh. Oh well. But it makes me think about all the decisions we make every day. What to wear. Do I put on new underwears today. Do I sleep a little bit more an catch da later bus.

Do I turn left. Do I turn right. Do I buy this. Do I eat dat. Boy der's too many. It's a woner some of us decide anythin' at all, eh. An dat's a decision too. Doin' nothin'. An it's easy to forget too, eh, that everythin' we decide has an effec. It's like dat game with da marbles an da plastic sticks. Ker plunk I tink dey call it. You pull out dat stick an it's OK. An maybe you pull dat stick an all da marbles fall. But it's the power of dat decision, eh. So whatever you guys decide today, whether it's big or small, jus remember dat it's one of our greatest gifts as human bein's, eh. The power to decide. You always got choice. Even if yer say decidin' between eatin' da black jelly bean, which you may hate, an da pink jelly bean, which you may hate more. Der's still choice der, eh. Sometimes we worry 'bout what's da right decision an we go "hmmm" an "I doan know…" An we forget to 'member how powerful choices make us, eh. Da decisions are like da underwears, eh. We got da power to change dem. Me. I ushely go with my firs instinc. 'Cause even if da firs "D's" not so good I still got two "D's left, eh. I'm Joe from Winnipeg. Meegwetch.

Rubber Boots

Hey you guys, this is me, Joe from Winnipeg. Today I'm gonna be talkin' to you 'bout rubber boots. But firs, I gotta say something again. I'm walkin' 'round da city da other day. Lookin' at stuff. Window shoppin'. Although I doan know why it's called dat. You doan actually shop for windows dat way, although dat would be a good way to know if it's da kine you like. An we can't buy what's behind da window, so…what's up with that? But anyways, I'm thinkin' 'bout things that are goin' on in da world, eh. An I can't figure out how everything got so imbalance. People killin' one anothers. People discussin' how many refugees to let in da country. Come on you guys. Most of yous is refugees or descendants of dem. Whether by choice or by force. I wish dese guys would learn dat you can't get possessive over a land you don't own. Nobody owns it. Right? An speakin' of dat, what's up with da premier? "I doan unerstand what dese people want." I can't believe I was gonna vote for dis guy. Maybe 'Nishnawbe will create alternative conservative party to split vote. Somethin like Reform party, 'cept less understandin'. Den if dey run in election da leader can say, "I doan unerstand what you voters want. So you should vote for me. 'Cause if I'm dis out of touch, 'magine how…" OK. I'm jus kiddin' der. Sorry 'bout dat. So. Rubber boots. OK. I figure I go buy new rubber boots, 'cause my ole ones had little tiny hole in der, eh. An da water collects in der an yer foot makes that "squish squish" soun, eh. I wore a plastic bag on my foot couple times but den I figured what's da point of havin' rubber boots if you need to wear waterproof lining for dem to work. So I went bought new ones. Good ting 'bout rubber boots. Dey're still pretty cheap. So I'm lookin' at dem in da store, wondrin' if I'll get da black ones with red tip. Or black one with green tip. Hmmm. Den I run into my frien who don't want me to name him. But he lives in big house an used to drive bright orange

Volkswagen Beetle, eh. An he's English. An he's goin' to someplace call Dubai. At first when he tole me he was goin' Dubai, I said "Dubai what?" "No. Dubai." "I know. Dubai what?" "Not what. Dat's da place." "What's da place?" "No. What's on second." Den he laughs. Boy it took me 'bout 15 minutes to fine out Dubai is a city in Middle East. "What you goin' der for?" I ask my unnamed English frien with a big house an used to have bright orange Beetle. "Oh I'm goin' window shoppin'." Yeah right. He's buyin' some cool clothes 'cause it's hot in dis Dubai place. Gotta stay comfortable, he tells me. So I wish him a good trip an I buy black rubber boots with green tips. Would have preferred da traditional rubber boots, but dey didn't have my size. So I can't wait to get home and put on my new rubber boots. An I go for walk. An I walk through all kines of puddles, eh. Der's something very liberatin' about dat. Walkin' through puddles. I highly recommend dat to you guys. An as I'm walkin' I tink. Hmmm. Dat's funny. I'm really only wearin' rubber boots for one reason eh. Comfort. An I think of all da tings in our lives dat we have for comfort. In fact, seems like most of what we do is for da comfort, eh. Whether dat's work to buy a nice chair, or however it is you take it easy. I guess you could even argue dat everythin in our lives an what motivates us has to do with tryin' to make ourselves comfortable, from my frien an his cool clothes to me an my rubber boots. We sure don't like cold, wet feets, eh? Maybe today when you realize one of da many tings dat makes you comfortable you can say little prayer for all dose people who aren't so comfortable. I'm Joe from Winnipeg. Meegwetch.

Piggybacks

Hey you guys, this is me, Joe from Winnipeg. Today I'm gonna be talkin' to you 'bout piggybacks. How you guys doin' today? Are you ready for everythin' that life's gonna throw at you? We never seem to be, eh, yet we manage somehow. What's up with that? So. Piggybacks. I was wondrin' 'bout dat word piggybacks. We all know what it means, but why is it called dat, eh? Why not horsiebacks? We sure ride dose more dan we do pigs. 'Cept my dad an his brother. When dey were boys on da farm dey had to look after dese two piglets. An dey did, but den dey started playin' with dem. Doin' wheelbarrow races with dem. An even gettin' for real piggybacks. Boy, came time to…well, you know what happens to pigs on da farm, an my dad an his brother couldn't eat dat dinner, eh. But evrybody was amaze at how lean dat meat was. So anyways, I seen dis young woman giving piggyback ride to a little boy, eh. An was dat ever sweet. I forgot all about piggybacks. Dat's funny how we can forget about something until we see it again. Like say, ole frens. Or pack of Freshie with da little bird on it. Even ole style box of Beep with little happy bird saying "beep" on der. Maybe dey'll bring dat back as baby boomer nostalgia. Classic Beep dey can call it. Anyways, I was 'membering how we used to play chicken fights. Where you piggyback somebody an you try knock each other down. 'Member dat game? Why it's called chicken fight I doan know. More like da bumping into each other till somebody falls over fight. An it's sad how much dat word "fight" is in tings we do. Maybe dat's why der's still so much stupid war goin' on among us human bein's. But I gotta say, I had fun playin' games like dat. Or givin' piggyback rides to people. Now yer wondrin'. What's da point of da piggyback ting, Joe? Well. Lots been goin' on, eh? Like I said. Life always throwin' stuff at us. Tings I doan understan, eh? Like da big one. Dis war dat's goin' on. They're still not callin' it dat yet. It's only "conflict" for now. Or da nurse strike in Saskatchewan. NDP government legislatin' workers back to work? I'm not arguin' ethics over dat, but dat would kine of be like Conservative government spendin' lots of money on healthcare and raising tax on business, eh. Know what I mean? An den here I'm readin' paper an I see dat relative of mine dies in jail. Again. Not blamin' anybody. But why do things like this keep happenin' to people? What's up with all of it? An den I tink. Boy. It'd be great if der was somebody to piggyback me through all dese questions, eh. All da rough spots in life. Don't have to worry 'bout question or answer. Just get piggyback through it. Life says, here's bad news, Joe. No problem. I got piggyback. Den I tink. Hey I do got piggyback in a way. Whether dat's friens. Family. Stranger. Prayer. Der's lots of way to get piggyback through rough spots, eh. So I hope you guys fine dose piggybacks to help you with what life throw at you, eh. Whatever it is. If it's person you see who's stronger dan you. Just jump on der back. Well not literal. You might hurt dem. Someone did dat to me an we both ended up like pancake on da groun. Mmmm. Pancake. An sausage. OK. Now I'm hungry. I'm Joe from Winnipeg. Meegwetch.

Odometer Checks

Hey you guys, this is me, Joe from Winnipeg. Today I'm gonna be talkin' to you 'bout odometer checks. I had to go drive somebody to Moosomin, Saskatchewan, eh. You guys ever been der? Nice place. Anyways, after my frien picked up der cheque I drove dem back to Winnipeg 'cause they always feel safer on the highway if somebody else is drivin'. I guess dat flattered me, 'cause I'm used to my passengers grabbin' da dash board and movin' der leg like dey're pushin' a brake. So anyways, we're drivin' home an my friend falls asleep. An I don't got much to do except drive an think. I didn't turn on da radio 'cause I didn't want to wake up my frien. An we're drivin' along da Trans Canada an I'm thinkin' 'bout things. Gettin' all contem plative. Or is it contemplative. I'm never sure 'bout dat. So I contemplated dat question for a while. An den I pass dis sign dat says odometer check one kilometre. An den another sign. Begin odometer check now. An for some reason I got paranoid, eh. It was just like I was takin' a test instead of a check. An I'm drivin' an tryin' to make sure da odometer's rollin' past da same number as I pass da signs dat say 1 kilometre. Or is it kilometre. Don't get distracted Joe. Two kilometre. An so on. An I see dat da seven comes up at about da same time for evry sign, but I'm not too sure 'cause I was tryin' to watch da road an da number an da sign at the same time eh. It was VERY hard, eh. An boy, if I didn't start contemplatin' life, eh. An dat's what dat odometer check is like. 'Cept da signs doan say kilometre so an so. Dey're tings like baby's bein' born. Graduatin' things. Maybe even doctor checkup, eh. Any little time we look aroun an go, "Yup. I doan really know what I'm doin'. But everythin seems OK." An it's always good to check an make sure yer life is goin' the way you want it to. 'Cause if it isn't. You're the driver. 'Member that. An for me, the thing I contempl…thought about was how come I'm so lucky that I get to talk to you peoples evry week.

I'm just a guy. An der's lots of peoples with same ideas, even better ones. All I can think is I'm s'posed to be doin' this. You know, for a long time Native people have had to struggle to be heard. Lots of us are still tryin' to find our voice, eh. How do we get heard? Are people listenin'? An I have to say yes. Some people are listenin'. An some people are doin' like da odometer checks on all of us all da time, eh. How come dese people are hungry? How come they're still so much war? What are we doin' about this? 'Cause thing I noticed too 'bout those odometer checks. We doan really need them. What if yer odometer don't work. Are you gonna stop yer car on da highway. Get out. Walk away. "Oh no. I can't ride in dat car. Da odometer don't work." It's just a good reminder for us that sometimes things need attendin' too. I'm Joe from Winnipeg. Meegwetch.

Canada

Hey you guys, this is me, Joe from Winnipeg. Today I'm gonna be talkin' to you 'bout Canada. I know I'm ushely more vague in the things I talk about, but then Canada's little bit vague sometimes so… Anyways, I was sittin' around contemplatin' my cereal and milk, eh. Like, how much milk is enough milk for cereal. Just a little bit, so the cereal dominates, or maybe a whole bunch so that the cereal's floatin', eh. Or should you have enough milk so there's some left to drink out of the bowl afterwards? An what if it's Fruit Loops, then the milk gets discoloured an more milky. Is dat possible? Milky milk. Souns like some kine of rapper. Anyways, as I was contemplatin' my milk cereal ratios I was readin' the box an at first I thought it said, "…if this product does not have enough meat for your expectations…" an I got kine of mad, eh. Hey, they're rippin' us consumers off, there's no meat in this cereal. Then I thought, wait a minute, that's a good thing. So I read it again an saw that it was meet with two e's, not an a, eh. Then I'm thinkin' that's a good thing I caught my mistake otherwise I would have been at the grocery store with my Corn Flakes sayin', "Where's the beef?" But I was able to avoid this huge misunderstandin' by double checkin' an applying some logic. So dat's what started me thinkin' 'bout Canada. 'Cause this whole country got its name from a misunderstandin', eh. I'm sure most of you know this story where they first come to Turtle Island an ask the 'Nishnawbe what this land is called, an they say, "Kanata." An the rest is a history. I mean, "an" history. There's been misunderstandin' goin' on before this nation was here, eh. An it's still goin' on today. Between diffrent peoples. 'Specially between the 'Nishnawbe an the rest of Canada. Nurses. All kines of workers actually. Misunderstandin' in famlies. Between friens. You name it. But I believe we're gonna work that out. We'll fine just the right mix of the milk an the cereal. Maybe realize that it's all a matter of personal taste anyways. I hope you guys avoid misunderstandin' in yer life today. An have a good time in this wonderful country that maybe should have had a different name, but then again, it works. Have a good summer. I'm Joe from Winnipeg. Meegewetch.

A Big Piece of Plastic

Hey you guys, this is me, Joe from Winnipeg. Today I'm gonna be talkin' to you 'bout a big piece of plastic. I gotta do dat 'cause I wasn't sure what to talk about at first. Der's so much goin' on. But den der's always so much goin' on. I guess dis time my ole big mouth could only say so much, eh. So. OK. Big mouth. Do yer stuff. Happy Birthday, Winnipeg. I know some peoples wanted a big party or a cake, but I think dat Winnipeg is actin' how most of us get when we get older, eh. Jus rather forget about da birthdays. Preten der just another day. I doan know, but to me, celebratin' community's a good ting. An I love dat I can say dat I'm Joe from "Winnipeg." Joe from someplace else would make me feel lost, eh. We got a new LG too eh. I'm tryin' to make dat soun more hip. I doan really know what a leftenant is. But I know what a governor is. Maybe some day we'll have a wrestler for our leftenant governor. Boy, den if I got to meet him he might give me a body slam instead of da hand shake. An say, "Der, is dat fake? Hunh?" I'm just kidding. An den der's da Clinton. You know dat whole mess jus proves one ting. We're always our own worse enemy, eh. Whether dat's a country. Or us individuals. An den all da pain an war in da Kosovo. You jus wanna cry an go, "What's up with dat?" An dis guy who buried hisself under da groun for 150 days or something. Livin' der with a TV an not much else. Dey call him da human mole. Dose English peoples is so polite. I know housin's always a problem, but why would you want to live in a box? What would ole Edgar Allen Poe tink, eh? An da new smokin' labels. Maybe dey should jus put a big ole dead rat on der with a circle an a line through him. Warning. Poison. SO. Big piece of plastic. I was watchin' dis big piece of plastic stuck in a tree, eh. It was twisted aroun part of it. An other parts were held by the branches. An once in a while da wind would catch it, eh. An puff it out like da back of our jackets on a windy day. An I thought, boy, dat ting is tryin' to escape from dat tree. But it prob'ly won't never happen. An den I thought, boy, dat big piece of plastic's kine of like us, eh. We're held together by many things. It's all very complex. An sometimes der's lots goin' on. An it's all very excitin'. An other times it's all relax, eh. Jus like all da stuff dat's goin' on. Rise an fall kine of. But da funny ting about watchin' dis big piece of plastic an tinkin' it's kine of like us an our lives. Big an small. Da ting we're tryin' to get away from is what's holdin' us together. Very strange dat. Boy. I'm even gonna mix up da metaphor an say dat we're da tree too, eh. Our community. Our histry. But da ting I noticed most about dis big piece of plastic in a tree was how beautiful it was, eh. I'm Joe from Winnipeg. Meegwetch.

Who's the Boss?

Hey you guys, this is me, Joe from Winnipeg. Today I'm gonna be talkin' to you 'bout who's the boss. I doan mean that sitcom with the Tony Danza an Judith Light. The one where he was an old taxi driver who was her maid or something like that. Didn't really make sense, 'cause you jus knew dat she was the boss. So I doan know how come they had a question mark on their title. Boy. Did you guys see the sunset the other night? I jus looked like somebody asked me how to fix a broken water main. My mouth was hangin' open. My eyes blinked a couple times. It was beautiful blues and greens and some other colour I doan know how to say. Anyways, I was standin' there an my frien Howie walks past me, eh. Mumbling something. Completely ignoring me. An he's holding something in his han. Lookin' at it. So I go to ask Howie what he's doin', an I hear him sayin', "Looks like plastic. But it feels like rubber." "What does?" I ask him. An he shows me this little thing he's holdin'. So I takes it an I go, "Hmmm. Does look like plastic an feel like rubber. Where'd you get it?" "My nose," he tells me. Ahhh. I'm jus kidding. But it was my frien Howie. An we tell each other all the excitin' things happenin' in our lives. "What's new with you?" "Nothin'. How 'bout you?" "Same." An den Howie says, "Oh. Der is somethin' new. My boss left us." An I ask him what he means, an den he tells me dat his boss jus took off. So who's the boss I ask him. An he says he don't know. But he's kine of scared, 'cause without a hierarchical structure at work he's afraid there's gonna be too many liberties. I tole him not to worry though. It's pretty hard to think of liberties an workin' for the government. But you know. All this worryin' 'bout who's the boss makes me think about this Wantonio Sam-a-ranch. Boy I have a hard time with dat guy's name. I wish he had a "ma" at the en of his name instead of a "nch" then he'd be Wantonio Samarama. Now I hear he had an extravaganza in the Japan. It could've been da Samarama 'Stravaganza. An they cooked da expense books in Nagano. Real literal eh. Dey burned them 'cause they say they didn't have no place to put them. Boy I fine dat one hard to buy, dat's when garbage bags come in handy as storage containers. Speakin' of buy. I guess dat's what started this whole thing. Buyin' the 'Lympics. An IOC people. I doan even know what dat IOC is. An when I wonder who's the boss, I know it's dat Samaranch guy. I think people want him to just take off too, eh. But why should he? He can just say what my nephew says when I tell him to go to bed, "You're not the boss of me." An I ushely scratch my head an tink, "He's right." I guess the one thing I learned 'bout this whole 'Lympic scandal thing is we all got a boss, eh. An dat's us. Next time someone asks you, "Who's the boss aroun here?" you can say, "Me." I just wish this Sam-a-ranch guy, who already knows he's the boss, would use dat power for good, instead of tryin' blow smoke with this new duping commission. Me. I'm gonna go look at da sky again to remine myself dat der's an even bigger boss over all of us, eh. Da weather. I'm Joe from Winnipeg. Meegwetch.

Screwballs

Hey you guys, this is me, Joe from Winnipeg. Today I'm gonna be talkin' to you 'bout screwballs. Boy, der's just so many screwballs I doan know where to begin. Let's start with da goverment. Aenhh. I'm just kidding. Dat's not da kine of screwballs I mean. Although der's sure plenty out der. Take yer pick, eh. I kine of like da word 'cause it's not too mean, eh. You can call somebody a screwball an it's little bit compliment. "Hey. You know what? Yer a screwball. I can't believe you did dat." An dey might smile an nod der head an say, "Yup. Dat's me. Screwball." People like bein' risky without bein' called da real negative names, eh. An hey. Speakin' of dat. I doan usheally do dis, but I gotta say someting. It's botherin' me too much. You know dis horrible, awful, messy ting dat's goin' on in da Kosovo. An sometimes I hear da newspeople usin' da words "ethnic cleansing". I wish dey wouldn't do dat, 'cause dey're instillin' dose thoughts in people's heads. Like dat's what's goin' on. "Ethnic cleansing." It's murder, you guys. An genocide. Not "ethnic cleansing." So OK. I'm finished about dat. Screwballs. Well da kine of screwballs I mean are da ones you can buy in da store in da ice cream section, eh. Dey're in a little plastic, see-through cone an dey usheually come with der own little wooden spoon, right der in da freezer, whole bunch of dem held together by elastic. An da ice cream inside is pink with da ribbons of other flavours in der, eh. Mmmm. Dey're good. But you know, dey're sometimes hard to fine, eh. Like on da weekend. I couldn't fine any screwballs so I ended up walkin'. An it's a beautiful day. An der's famly's out rakin' der yards. Pullin' up all dose brown leaves an makin' sure da grass is breathin' again. An I see people walkin' der dogs. An some people jus walkin'. An I walk some more an I en up near dat BDI place, eh. An der's a whole bunch of people der buyin' ice cream. Boy, at last, I said. Here it is still pretty cold in da Manitoba an der's a bunch of people buyin' ice cream. I tink I found my screwballs. I'm jus kiddin'. I love dat us people in Manitoba is so desprate for spring to get started dat we start buyin' ice cream en of March, eh. I even saw people outside on restraunt patios too, eh. I guess da spring an all dat means is really here. An dat's good. I tink my favrit part is when we do da tings where we're peelin' away da stuff we doan need an showin' what's underneath, all da fresh an good stuff. Jus like da screwballs, eh. I findly foun one an boy was it good. An you know, der in da bottom was da prize, eh. Piece of gum. Dat's been sittin' in dat ice cream for who knows how long. You almos break yer teeth on it if yer not careful. I hope you guys fine da important tings you need in yer lives dis week. Da stuff dat's under all dat other stuff we pile on top, like work an jobs, an worryin' an gettin' stressed. Underneath all dat is somethin' real good. An maybe even join res of us screwballs who is lookin' for ice cream outside even dough der's still snow on da groun, eh. I'm Joe from Winnipeg. Meegwetch.

Towels

Hey you guys, this is me, Joe from Winnipeg. Today I'm gonna be talkin' to you 'bout towels. But firs, are you guys ready to not buy da gasoline tomorrow? Big protes against da oil companies or somethin'. I heard one guy say, "It's not gonna work, 'cause we need our cars." Funny. How we accep dat statement, yet we hardly ever hear somebody sayin' I need my partner. Or I need my children. What's up with that? I doan know. Personal, I doan think any of us needs cars. I'm talkin' 'bout towels 'cause I realized strange thing, eh. I was invited to little gatherins at two seprate friens houses, eh. So I go an dey're both pleasant events. An both of dem had one thing in common. Dey both used towels for curtains in da bathroom. In both cases it wasn't too professional job, eh. Dey jus sort of stuck dem on da window an stuffed dem into da little gap between da two parts of da window. Now I doan mean to be critical, but I got lots of experience hangin' tings in windows dat ain't supposed to be der, eh. Like sheets. An even flags, eh. I never had da kine dat was confederate flag or nothin' dough. Jus mosely da kine of flags dats from ole rock groups, eh. One ting 'bout hangin' towels in da bathroom window I taught wasn't too bad idea was dat you could jus get out of da bath or da shower an der you go. You always got a towel der. Now dat would only be in case you didn't have dose towel hanger tings, which by da way I wish dey would make extra strength, eh, 'cause I doan know how many of dose I've ripped off da wall tryin' to use dem for support. Anyways, I tink dat's good double use of towel in da bathroom an as long as you be discreet anybody lookin' in on you would be disappointed, eh. But dis get me thinkin' maybe we could use tings from da rooms where we live as tings to cover windows, eh. Kine of like theme decoratin'. So you got bedsheets in da window in da bedroom. An couchcover or cushions in da livin' room. Tinfoil or da waxpaper in da kitchen.

'Cept I'm not too sure 'bout hallway near front door. You wouldn't get much privacy from pair of boots or ole runners hangin' in dose windows. An I'm not sure 'bout nurseries. Diapers are kine of only good for one ting, eh. An hey. You guys hear 'bout dis guy who invented new fire retard gel? It's made out of same stuff dey make out of diapers. He gets inspired by goin' to dump where dey're burnin' stuff an he notices dat diapers aren't burnin', eh. I'm kine of glad to know dose tings are indestructible, eh, but why did dey need to make dem fire resist? So anyways dis guy figures, Hey. I'll make da fire retard gel out of dat. I'm glad he didn't tink of makin' house out of da diaper material, eh. Or no-stick cookin' utensil. Or even firepeople's clothes. Dey do important job for us an I doan wanna picture dem slidin' down dat pole in diapers. Boy, I guess I'm demonstratin' how dangerous it is when idea goes too far, eh. But towels. People usin' towels as curtains makes me tink. Dis shows to me how resourceful we all are. I'm Joe from Winnipeg. Meegwetch.

Eatin' with Strangers

Hey you guys, I'm Joe from Winnipeg. Today I'm gonna be talkin' to you 'bout eatin' with strangers. I guess dat happens evry time we go in a restraunt, eh? But sometimes in other strange places too. Ole Joe was on an airplane a little while ago. Which I foun to be pretty much like da bus. Noisy an cramped. But dey did feed me. You only get dat if you feed yerself on da bus. So, der I was stuck in the middle an I was eatin' der like dis. Lookin' forward pretendin' I was thinkin' about somethin'. But really I was thinkin' how strange dis is dat I'm eatin' with strangers, eh. I bet dose guys were thinkin' the same ting. I say dat 'cause dey were bein' discreet with der elbows too, eh. I never realized I needed so much elbow room to eat. But you know what? I couldn't take dat much more, eh. Eatin' with strangers. So I introduced myself an said hello. I had jus become da guy on da plane who tells you his life story. An for you guys nex time you fine yerself eatin' with strangers, maybe even at yer own dinner table, maybe try talkin'. I'm Joe from Winnipeg. Meegwetch.

Senses

Hey you guys, this is me, Joe from Winnipeg. Today I'm gonna be talkin' to you 'bout senses. I just gotta say meegwetch and thank yous to you guys for lettin' me talk with you some more. It means very much to me, an I'll do my bes to do my bes. OK then. Senses. So the other day I'm riding my bike around, and I'm thinkin', "Hey. Maybe I should ride my bike to the bus stop an fine one of those buses with the bike racks on the front, so I can take the bus and get even less exercise than walkin'." Nah. Too much convenience can be bad thing, eh. Look at what happen with channel nine. I went out of town for little bit and I get back and there's people talkin' on channel nine. No comfort music. No two-tone green an red. How am I s'posed to 'just the hoo an colour on my channels now whenever someone in my famly decides to mess aroun with it? That was very useful channel in more ways than one an they go an change it without askin' us. Anyways, I went for a ride on my bike. Jus to ride aroun. An it was so pleasant. Little bit scary too, 'cause I was in one of the suburbs of the city an I figured I'd go get Slurpee, eh. So I go to the Sev there an hoa wah, was there ever a bunch of wasps hangin' aroun, eh. All in front of the store. An people was scared to go inside the Sev 'cause of all these wasps, eh. I guess they got a right to do dat, but they shouldn't be terrorizin' us poor potential customers. So. I kept ridin' 'cause I didn't want to get stung, eh. An I'm ridin' aroun a bit. Lookin' at the leaves starting to change. An I smell some of the last barbecues of qhe millennium here in Winnipeg. An I ride over some crab apples an they go "sqwutch," eh. An then some acorns too, an they kine of "pop." An then I get little bit wet from some guy washin' his minivan with da hose. Boy dat guy was way out of han, he even hosed down stroller an car seat, eh. An I heard a famly enjoyin' each other's company. Then I smell some fresh cut grass. Boy I even thought I smelled some sweet grass der. All good this stuff. An all gifts we can enjoy 'cause of our senses, eh. Whether that's the touch of some water. Taste of crab apple. Smell of nice barbecue. Hearin' people visitin'. Or seein' the leaves starting to change, eh. Boy, even that six sense that tells you things you couldn't possibly know. Or maybe just to trust yerself. An that's what I hope you guys do as the seasons start to change. An it gets cold again. An our senses get to feel diffrent, but familiar things, eh. Like crunchy leaves an 'ventually minus thirty. Trust that you an the people you love are gonna be OK. An boy too there's gonna be 'lection here in Manitoba. Our chance to exercise our choice over the second level of government in dis country. As I just foun out we in Canada are considered a fedral state, eh. For years I thought we was a compound republic, but doan get me started on that. I'm just glad I got senses that was made in Manitoba, 'cause there's lots to experience an decide, eh. An all dese tings involve our senses. You guys have a good day. I'm Joe from Winnipeg. Meegwetch.

Chemistry

Hey you guys, this is me, Joe from Winnipeg. Today I'm gonna be talkin' to you 'bout chemistry. How are yous? Good I hope. I'm more than fine, but less than great. So I'm not sure what the word for that is. Copeseptic maybe. Anyways, I hope you guys doan get mad at me, but I'm gonna 'courage you to vote. Even if you jus go in der to mess up yer ballot 'cause yer not happy with yer choices. I think you should exercise dat privledge of votin'. Although, sometimes votin's like buying new shirt. What you really want ain't der, eh, but you gotta make a choice, an maybe it's wrong colour an wrong size, but you can live with it. So OK, anyways, chemistry. I'm thinkin' 'bout chemistry 'cause of lots of reasons. I was lookin' at da sky, eh. An I know Jupiter's up der somewhere. Dis big planet dat's made up of some kine of gases, like you fine in balloons and comin' out of cows. An on dat planet is da big red dot, eh. An dat dot is like two times as big as da earth. An it's some kine of storm. An now we got a big dot of our own here, eh. Called Hurricane Floyd. An is dat ting ever huge. Six hunerd miles I hear. Six hunerd! Dat's way more than from here to Thompson. Or even from Winnipeg to Thunder Bay. It's all very scary. And I doan mean to sound careless, but I'm glad we don't get hurricanes in Winnipeg or Thompson or Thunder Bay. But we can pray for those people in those areas that them an their homes and famlies will be OK. So the other thing about chemistry I was thinkin' was because of this nice chemistry couple I met. His name was Frank. Hers was Donna. And he was tellin' me a story 'bout how he was workin' in the lab late one night an he blew his nose and put the Kleenex in his pocket, eh. Then he said he put this vial of stuff, potassium percolate or somethin' in the same pocket. So he's goin' 'bout his work there mixin' chemicals an he happens to notice his pocket's on fire, eh. Big flames shootin' out of his pocket. 'Cause I guess this potassium reacted with the wet

Kleenex. Boy, if I was a chemical person I'd hate to have to worry about my pockets catching fire all the time. Very annoying. Anyways, Donna, Frank's wife, said that this was just his way of tryin' to say that he was "hot." Maybe eh, but that's a little bit too much of the extreme to me. I would just do somethin' with cinnamon hearts those are "hot." Anyways, I'm talkin' 'bout all this diffrent kind of chemistry 'cause there's so many diffrent kines of it, eh. An it works in so many diffrent ways. It can make storms that remine us who's the boss of this planet. An the same potassium that's good for you in bananas can catch fire in yer pocket if you got wet Kleenex. An all the other chemistry you got in yer life is there to enrich it, eh. Whether that's people you got the chemistry with or even the chemistry you're gonna make today. All of it makes the world and the people on it go 'round, eh. I'm Joe from Winnipeg. Meegwetch.

Flounders

Hey you guys, this is me, Joe from Winnipeg. Today I'm gonna be talkin' to you 'bout flounders. You guys ever seen these kine of fishes? They got two eyes on one side of their head, 'cause they live on the bottom of the ocean. What's up with that? Did their one eye get sick of lookin' at the bottom of the sea all the time, figure, "This is borin'. I'm gonna migrate to the other side of my head, see what's goin' on"? Which really makes me wonder how they see their food, eh. They must just taste everythin' an then decide if they wanna eat that or not. Anyways, reason I'm talkin' 'bout flounders is 'cause I got asked strangest question. I was sittin' down on a bench in one of the shopping malls, admirin' all the glass and water fountains and trees, then this woman started talkin' to me. She mistaked me for someone else, but once she started talkin' to me she kept goin'. Anyways, she asked me if I knew her brother Kelly from the Braintree, eh. She say he's "bad rarin'," whatever that means, but still a nice guy. An this is where the strange question happens. She wants to buy him present, eh. So she asked my advice. I say, "Buy him nice watch maybe. Or else somethin' from the dollar store. They got nice little things made of plastic in der. An all kines of things you never knew you needed, eh. Like vegtable scrubbers an keychains made out of horseshoe nails." "No. No. I wanna get him a fish," she says to me. "Ohhhh. What kine?" I ask her. "Either a halibut or a flounder. But I can't tell which is which. Do you know if the eyes are on the left side if it's a halibut? Or if they're on the right they're a flounder?" I doan know, I says to her. "Oh well," she says an walks away. An that's the strange question I got asked. Then I foun out that these fishes have two eyes on one side of their head an live on the ocean bottom. I was very confused thinkin' about this. Just like I've been very confused over what's goin' on with the 'Nishnawbe fishermens an the white fishermens on the east coast.

The one side upset 'cause the Native fishermens can fish out of season. The other side doin' what the treaty they signed said they could do. An this is where I get real confused, eh. I en up bein' like those fish. I can see both sides of the arguments. From the left side and the right side. Bein' 'Nishnawbe myself I know how Native peoples have had much taken away from them. An why were those treaties signed in the first place if they're not gonna be honoured? Which is what's happenin' now. An so now the non-Native fishermens are mad 'cause it's not fair the Indians get this and not them. I'm very confused eh. 'Cause in my head, I'm goin', "Yes. I see yer point der. An on da other side, I go, Yes. I see yer point der too. Both very good points." An I go round an round like that in my head. It's all so complex, eh. But then I think…no. Nope. It's not really complex. It's very simple. It's like the halibut an the flounder. We got diffrent views. Sometimes we see from the left side of the head. Sometimes the right. Sometimes right in the middle. An all of the tensions an anger can be dealt with. Talked about an understood, eh. Sos we don't end up flounderin', but thrivin'. I'm Joe from Winnipeg. Meegwetch.

Mixed Vegetables

Hey you guys, this is me, Joe from Winnipeg. Today I'm gonna be talkin' to you 'bout mixed vegetables. At first I thought I was gonna talk about niblets or Brussels sprouts, but they get too much attention as it is eh. One's got cute name. Niblets. An other's got exotic name. Brussels sprout. Even in vegetable world, life can seem so unfair, eh. Hey, you guys catch the throne speech the other day? Was that excitin' or what, hunh? Heard it all before maybe. I was thinkin' instead of readin' it from a throne they could maybe try diffrent themes. Like easy chair speech. Or rockin' chair speech. Maybe even speech from the barber chair. Then somebody, like Prime Minister maybe, could play with the height adjustment there. Make the Govner Genral go real high for extra effect. And make her spin aroun for all the fun stuff in the throne speech, like…hmmm. Anyways, mixed vegetables. Other day we had the Thanksgivin', eh. An evrybody in my famly had to cook somethin'. Me. I had to cook the mixed vegetables. An boy, let me tell you. That's not as easy as you think. For me anyways. I'm the kine of cook who has to let machine do it for me, eh. Like microwave. Or toaster. Only things I use stove for is boil water to make tea or wieners. Toast with hanger if toaster's bust. An sometimes extra heater when it's cold, eh. So anyways, I was readin' the instructions on the bag of mixed legooms. I like the French word for vegtable little bit better. Could've even been failed ad campaign, eh. "Hey. Legoom my lima beans." "Sure. You can have it." "Kids just hate the taste of lima beans. So make sure you trick them into eatin' them. Or make sure they can't leave the table till they're done." Anyways, I'm such a bad cook. I had to read instructions for cookin' the mixed vegetables, eh. You know anybody who's got to read instruction for boilin' stuff is dangerous to have in kitchen. So it say on there, "How to stovetop steam." And in BIG letters: PLACE frozen vegetable in pan an boil.

REDUCE heat and cook accordin' to chart. DRAIN and serve immediately. And there was this chart there, eh, for how many people you have an how much water to use. How long to cook it. Oh was I ever confused. 'Cause I didn't know how much was too much, eh. I like havin' turkey leftover, but not mixed vegetable. You reheat them an it's kine of like they're sayin', "Uh unh. You missed yer chance. You should've had me yesterday." But you know, other thing these mixed vegetables make me think of is, that six billionth person that got born. You hear that number, six billion, an it goes in one side of the head an out the other. Just like throne speech. But it's scary too. Is there too much of us human bein's on the planet? How do we know if there's too much? An if there is too much what can we do about it? An why are most of them poor? An why if there's only thirty million of us in Canada are some of us complainin' about a few refugees? I doan know. The thing I take comfort in all the questions is that we're all connected, eh. To each other. An we're all diffrent too. Like the mixed vegetables. Some of us like corn. Some lima beans. Some of us can cook. Some can't. Maybe some of the answer's like lovin' someone too, eh. There's no such thing as too much. I'm Joe from Winnipeg. Meegwetch.

Copper

Hey you guys, this is me, Joe from Winnipeg. Today I'm gonna be talkin' to you 'bout copper. How you guys doin' today? You all bushy eyed an bright tailed? I hope so, since I can't really hear your response, but I pretend I can. I guess it would kine of be scary if you could talk to the radio. I really like bein' able to talk to you guys, but I got little bit mixed up the other day. This nice lady says to me, "Are you Joe? Oh I listen to you every mornin'." Evry mornin'? What's up with that? I'm only on once a week. An if she listens to me evry mornin' that mus be some other Joe she's hearin'. Then I figured, she's prob'ly just confusin' me with Terry McLeod, which I can unerstand 'cause we got simlar accents. You shouldn't listen to someone evry mornin' anyways, just yer tummy maybe. Arrr roow. Feed me. Isn't that great how yer stomach can embarrass you if you doan treat it right? So anyways, copper. I'm talkin' 'bout that 'cause it seems to be on evrybody's mind lately eh. See, I met this real nice couple Mrs. an Mr. Melnyk. We was waitin' in line to buy little bit of food. An we got to chattin' an they were tellin' me war stories, eh. Not from their marriage, but from the world war two. Like 'bout the 'Nishnawbe guy from Fisher Branch who could speak Ukrainian. Made me wish I could speak more Ukrainian, all I can say is bitaemo, an I learned that at the Folklorama. Anyways, I get my change. An it's a penny, eh. An Mrs. Melnyk says to me, "You could buy lots with a copper. Now people throw them away." An what she said hit me. 'Cause I forgot that we used to call pennies copper. An they kine of have become meaningless now, eh. You can't even buy mojo anymore with them. An the only reason some of us keep them is so we can give exact change. But they are still a help to lots of charities, eh. Those little boxes by cash registers. But the other thing 'bout copper is it used to be used by 'Nishnawbe long time ago, eh. It was used in trade. An we were gonna be usin' it in developin' new computer chip technology but figured, nah, what the world needs now is more love less technology. Anyways, I see many people bein' worried about trade right now. Like the sale merger whatever of all the airplanes in Canada. This kine of seems like the bank merger thing to me. Less choice ushely means more money to be paid. An lots of other people I talk to are worried 'bout money, eh. "Oh I hate livin' from cheque to cheque." "There's never enough." "Why can't I save more." All kines of things. I kine of wish it would be a bit more like Mrs. Melnyk said, eh. Make all this money meaningless. They talk about hunerds of millions and billions of dollars an it is meaningless, eh. Yet so many times we make it the most important things in our lives. They say money makes the world go 'round, but it's people that do that. Not money. I like to think of the money like copper sometimes, eh. It can be very useful. Like in wires an in our pockets as change, but really it's only as important as we make it. I'm Joe from Winnipeg. Meegwetch.

Eclipses

Hey you guys, this is me, Joe from Winnipeg. Today I'm gonna be talkin' to you 'bout eclipses. I know we had one this summer, but it's still got me thinkin'. Hey. You guys hear 'bout dese women who wanna sell eggs for fifty thousan dollars? What's up with that? Unless that's Fabergee egg I wouldn't pay fifty thousan dollars. See, thing with eggs is you never quite know what yer gonna get. You got pretty good idea, but yer never sure till you crack it open. An I really doan think that's too ethical sellin' eggs for fifty thousan dollars. Maybe dey'll cost dat much in the far future when we no longer live on the surface an drive cars like the Jetsons, but for now I'll keep payin' reasonable price for eggs. An buy them from the farmer or the supermarket. So anyways, eclipses. What's got me thinkin' 'bout that is the strange coincidences that's been happenin' in my life, eh. Well, some people call them coincidences, I call them meant to happen. Here's the biggest meant to happen. Last week I get to go to Calgry for one day, eh. These guys asked me to come talk to them about how to get good night's sleep an since I'm real good at sleepin' I said sure. Anyways, there's all these people there that was walkin' aroun in robes, cup of coffee an newspaper in their hans. Oh I felt so sorry for them. Some of them was insomniacs, some so stressed they just couldn't sleep. So I teach them how to count sheep to sleep an read real borin' books like *Activity-Based Cost Management. Making It Work: A Manager's Guide to Implementing and Sustaining an Effective ABC System*. Well, I doan if that book's that borin' I ushely fall asleep before I read it, but it's about accountin', so…Anyways, I sit down an start talkin' to this guy next to me. An we talk a bit an fine out we both live in Winnipeg. An then we fine out we live on the same street. An then we fine out we're neighbours. Wow. What's up with that? I'm thinkin'. I gotta come all the way to Calgry to meet my neighbour. Where would I have to go to meet the other tenants in the house, eh. But of course we doan have to travel a thousan miles to meet somebody who lives a few feet away. But I guess if we're s'posed to hook up with that person we will. It's just a little bit frightening to go so far to meet someone who lives so near. An that's why it kine of makes me think of eclipse. 'Cause you ever wonder why in total solar eclipse the moon is just the right size to cover the sun? If the moon was little bit closer or little bit further away it would be very diffrent. Now what's up with that? Maybe another reminder there's bigger things goin' on than we know. An that the people we need come into our lives when we need them. Whether that's new friends or old ones we lost touch with, eh. We hook up an make a good match. Just like the sun an the moon. 'Cause eclipses are beautiful, mouth hangin' open kine of things, eh. I hope you guys fine the people you need today. An hey, you wanna know somethin' more strange? When me an my neighbour meet up he's just as surprised as me at our meetin' an says, "Wow, Joe. What's up with that?" Now, What is up with that? I'm Joe from Winnipeg. Meegwetch.

Policy

Hey you guys, this is me, Joe from Winnipeg. Today I'm gonna be talkin' to you 'bout policy. But first, let me ask you, are you unhappy with yer job? Maybe the only thing keepin' you there is tellin' yerself yer lucky to have a job. Maybe you got a job an you don't get paid for it, like bein' a mommy or a daddy or even the child of somebody. Well, I wish I knew how people could be happy at their jobs, but we gotta work, eh. Whatever our job is. Only thing I can suggest is you find one thing you like about your job. Anything. For me when I got hatin' my job pumpin' gas I found that I liked goin' home after a shift. But that's not good advice. Hey, uh oh. I'm givin' advice too early here. So anyways, policy. Other day I'm talkin' to my frien, who I like a lot. An we get talkin' 'bout treatin' friends right. 'Cause we saw a TV show where somebody was s'posed to meet their friend for dinner, but went on a date at last minute, eh. Anyways, I figured that's forgiveable, eh. 'Cause who knows, maybe they might like each other an even smooch. But my frien says you never treat a friend like that. 'Specially if you made plans. So I asked my frien, what if I had tickets to say wrestlin' or a tractor pull an I showed up to surprise you, but you already made plans with another friend? An my frien says, nope. No way. As much as I might want to see wrestlin' (which is for real by the way) or even a tractor pull (which by the way is one of the best sports as example of form an function, 'cause what else is a tractor good for if not pullin', eh?), but my friend says, "No, Joe. Sorry. I have a policy. I would not do that to my friend." An I started to laugh. A policy? On how you treat yer friends? What's up with that? I asked her, what committee came up with this, eh? Maybe you could send me memo so's I'm aware of dis policy. Maybe make think tank to examine dis policy. But after I made fun I realized, Hey. Dat's not a bad policy. Treatin' yer friends good. An do I need more policies in my life? Like makin' sure I 'member to put the butter away so the cat don't lick it. Or makin' sure I have a policy where I acknowledge everyone who acknowledges me, eh. An den I realize I had funny reaction 'cause dat word policy can be 'nother word for conscience, eh. Or a reminder that we need rules sometimes to be good to each others. I guess that's why governments have them too. Not that they always follow them anyways, but I hope you guys create policies that work for you. Whether that's bein' good to friends or makin' sure you eat one meal with yer famly with no TV or even radio, eh. I'm Joe from Winnipeg. Meegwetch.

The Santa Job

Hey you guys, this is me, Joe from Winnipeg. Today I'm gonna be talkin' to you 'bout da unity debate. It's kine of gettin' to be like arguin' over a Creator. It just goes roun an roun an you end up havin' yer own opinion on it anyways, eh. I'm just kidding about talkin' 'bout that. I'm talkin' to you today 'bout the Santa job. An hey, what's up with these kooky scientists, eh? As if transplantin' heads wasn't enough, now they go an discover why we got two nostrils. You guys hear dis? I always thought it was sos we could have a choice of places to pick, eh. Or maybe it was nature's way of helpin' out all the left handin' peoples, sos they wouldn't have to pick at a funny angle. 'Course I tink we'd look pretty funny if we just had one nose hole, kine of like da tin man in *The Wizard of Oz*. 'Course he didn't use his nose, 'cause then he'd be singin' if I only had a nose, BUT anyways, the reason we got two nostrils is 'cause it seems they each smell diffrent things better, eh. Like maybe yer left nostril smells coffee real good an the right one smells cookies real good. So anyways, the Santa job. See, my brother got this job fillin' in for Santa for one night, eh. I guess Santa's a very busy guy an he needs some help sometimes. So my brother says to me, "Joe, what am I gonna do? I doan know nothin' 'bout bein' Santa." An I tell him, "Just be yerself. But preten yer Santa." Poor guy, I guess it wasn't enough me givin' him a complex when we're growin' up, now I'm givin' him another one. So a few days later I call to see how he's makin' out, eh. An my sister answers da phone. An we talk an I hear in da background, "Ho ho ho. Happy New Year. I mean Merry Christmas." An I figure my brother's gonna do okay at his Santa job, eh, even dough he was really unsure about what to do. Or even how to do it. Now, here's da ting. Child poverty in dis country is goin' up. Now instead of one million poor kids, der's one point four million poor kids. An maybe you hear dat an tsk tsk an shake yer head, but it's like da Santa job, eh. An I know some people even argue over Santa an what he represents, but what is Santa's job? Really? Makin' kids happy. Givin' to them, right? Whether dey're naughty OR nice. An what's so hard about dat? You know, it's kine of like my brother, eh. When we hear der's a job we gotta do we get kine of excited an den sometimes we get unsure of ourselves. "Oh no. What am I gonna do? Dat's too hard. I'm just one person." But I think dat's enough. Christmas is comin' soon. So, I hope you guys fine a small way to help out Santa, whether dat's givin' a penny to organization that helps kids, writin' a letter, or even usin' both nostrils to stop an smell dis problem. 'Cause it stinks. I'm Joe from Winnipeg. Meegwetch.

Kitty Litter

Hey you guys, this is me, Joe from Winnipeg. Today I'm gonna be talkin' to you 'bout kitty litter. I know, I know, sometimes what I'm talkin' 'bout is a little bit weird, but then sometimes the world is weird, eh. Like poor old Ben Johnson testin' positive again. Boy oh boy, this guy's like my cousin Jim. That guy can't help hisself when it comes to makin' the bed. I know that seems like a good thing, but if yer like me an you don't always want yer bed made it can be annoyin'. 'Cause I figure I'm just gonna sleep on it again in a few hours eh. Maybe he gets that from bein' in the military, but he comes to visit an you look in yer room later an yer bed's made. "Hey Jim. Did you make my bed?" Sometimes he admits to it, sometimes he lies an says "no." An then we start to talk about the bed makin' fairy. An how he must be short guy with a moustache wearin' sweats an pot belly, lookin' suspiciously like Jim. But he just can't seem to stop that behavior eh. An speakin' of behavior, poor ole Elton John. The guy gets upset 'cause the customs is holdin' him up? What's up with that? Welcome to Manitoba, Elton, yer lucky you weren't comin' in at Emerson on long weekend. Anyways, kitty litter. I was talkin' to my new frien Elaine, eh. An we were talkin' about many things. Like how she's startin' a new era in her life, eh. Movin' here from B.C. for the first time an bringin' all the warm weather with her. Boy, you know, elders always surprise me with their wisdom about life, eh. Showin' it's never too late to make a big change an to embrace that when that's what you choose to do, eh. An then we start talkin' about our favrit small animals. Like shrews. Moles. Hummin' birds. An all kines of baby animals too. 'Specially kittens. 'Cause dey're soooo cute, eh. I know some peoples like dogs an not cats an vice versus, but I really like both. It's just this time in my life I'm cat person eh. But I gotta control myself there too, 'cause other day I thought my kitten was talkin' to me an I started gettin' ideas like I might knit some mittens for my kitten, but what if she lost dem. Anyways, Elaine was givin' me advice about kitty litter. 'Cause der's all diffrent kines now, eh. Scented an unscented. Clumpin' an non-clumpin'. In a bag. In plastic container. Ho boy. An den I asked her why she liked kittens. An she tole me 'cause dey can take care of themselves. You doan need to take them for a walk an they can learn how to use kitty litter without too much fuss. An dat's da lesson I took from dat for my life eh. Knowin' when to take care of myself. 'Cause you know you can get so busy runnin' aroun doin' things, tryin' to help people, take care of yer famly, whatever. An before you know it, yer rundown, eh. Exhausted. An den yer no good to nobody. Not even yerself. Dat's what you gotta take care of yerself too. However you do dat. Maybe readin' a book. Havin' a hot bath. Or even makin' beds an cleanin' up if that's what you like. So whatever you do, do it for you. An sometimes our life is like kitty litter itself too, eh. It needs changin' from time to time. I'm Joe from Winnipeg. Meegwetch.

Patrols

Hey you guys, this is me, Joe from Winnipeg. Today I'm gonna be talkin' to you 'bout patrols. The kind that stand on the corner and make sure kids cross the street safe. Not the kind that wanders around lookin' for whatever. But hey, what's up with this Chretien? They supposedly made up a new improved War Measures Act. What's up with that? I'm not so crazy about the first one, so I don't know why they need to improve it. Kind of like improving cod liver oil to me. Now tastes worst. You may not like it, but we think it's good for you. They say it's in case anything happens with Y2K. I don't know about you guys, but I'm not sure what to believe. One hand, they say everything's gonna be fine, BUT just in case…they got backup plan. You know, in case there's riots, civil unrest, genral chaos. Remines me a little bit of my uncle who kept tellin' me, between cough fits, not to start smokin'. I welcome Y2K, eh. Bring it on. Anyways, patrols. Reason why I'm talkin' 'bout patrols, is 'cause I saw some the other day. There was four of them, and it was a three cornered thing, eh. One corner left empty. But they was talkin' to each other over traffic, holdin' those little orange flags and adjustin' their safety vests, eh. Doin' their duty. Makin' sure their classmates make it to an from school safely. Well. Funny thing happened to me. Smiled when I saw these patrols and what they're doin'. Thought, they're not really patrols, but more like people who stand on the corner and make sure you cross safe. And then I remembered. Remembered that I used to be a patrol. Back when the vests were just replacin' our little belts that we used to wear. And the flags were brand new then too, eh. And then I tried to remember why I wanted to be a patrol. To get out of class early? Nope. That benefit was overweighed by the fact that you always got home late for lunch. Was it the prestige and ability to "report" kids that didn't listen to you? Nope. Other kids always seemed to listen to you. Even seemed to trust us. So what was it? Truth is, I couldn't think why, eh? But these patrols I saw the other day, I believe they were doin' it 'cause they want to make a small diffrence, eh. Be good kids. Not 'cause they have to, but 'cause they want to, eh. Maybe not even bein' conscious of that. I guess what I'm seein' in these young people's example is that we don't have to know why we want to do somethin' good. Don't even have to think twice about it. Sure don't have to make no list and check it twice, findin' out who's naughty or nice. Just go for it, eh. 'Cause that goodness you do, will find its way back to you. I'm Joe from Winnipeg. Meegwetch.

Singin'

Hey you guys, this is me, Joe from Winnipeg. Today I'm gonna be talkin' to you 'bout singin'. Boy, I'm sure glad the snow's here, eh. I like feelin' the cold comin' off the windows, make me wanna bundle up, drink hot chocolate and wait to be discovered for some kind of commercial. Maybe one where they sell Internet stuff. You know, where your cold, metal computer can make you feel just like yer all bundled up, drinkin' hot chocolate. I hear most people ever are buyin' Christmas presents over the internet this year. I hate to say it, but I don't think I'd buy somethin' like say socks without bein' able to touch it and feel it in my hand. I never bought stuff out of catalogues neither. 'Cause one time that I did that, I bought underwears and I didn't look nothin' like the guy in the picture. Big smile. Hair that looked like Barbie doll Ken. Prob'ly just as hard. And lookin' at his watch, eh. Anyways. Singin'. You guys hear 'bout Julie Andrews. She's suin' a hospital that operated on her vocal cord. Now she can't sing no more. That's awful. 'Cause I think she has a beautiful voice, eh. And I'm sure she even knows how to sing in key. I figured out I couldn't do that when I was invited to share in celebratin' Christmas at Oxford church, eh. So there I was singin' away. People on either side of me lookin' at me funny. Then sort of smile. Keep on singin'. It was great, eh. Thing that struck me though. Here I was singin' this one Christmas carol, "It Came upon the Midnight Clear." And since I had a book in front of me, I was actually singin' the whole carol, eh. Not just the first part or the chorus and then goin' "na na na" for the rest of it. And boy, some of these carols have beautiful verses, eh. That one had real nice third verse. So after we all had a good time, talkin', tellin' stories and singin', I went home. Felt real good. In fact, it made me feel so good I still feel good, almost whole week later eh. I guess I didn't even know that I forgot that I could sing. Maybe not very good, by say

Julie Andrews standard, but I can sing. I was even takin' encouragement from my friend Maddy who plays music and sings all the time. Even when she's goin' to get drink of water, I hear she sees the piano, stops and plays some music. Then remembers she's thirsty and goes gets the water. Thing about all this singin'. I realized we don't do it nearly enough, eh. Some of us do. But most of us don't. And it's so easy to do. Especially if you're with lots of other people then you can sing as loud as you want. Even if you're off key like me, they may look at you, but they'll still smile. So I hope you guys do lots of singin'. Of evrythin', eh. Songs. Other people's praises. Even with the radio. Don't worry if you look funny to other drivers or people lookin' into your window, it's not for them you're singin'. It's for you. I'm Joe from Winnipeg. Meegwetch.

No Name Present

Hey you guys, this is me, Joe from Winnipeg. Today I'm gonna be talkin' to you 'bout the no name present. Man oh man, there's still so much goin' on in the world, eh. All the time. Good news and bad news. More flooding and Winnipeg bein' called the capital of Canada for something again. This time it's youth crime. Boy oh boy, I know our community has problems, but we're workin' on them. I've been to many places and this is still one of the best places to live. Raise a famly. Be happy. How come they don't ever say Winnipeg's the perogy capital of Canada. Or the Christmas lights capital of Canada. I bet if we did, there'd be people tryin' to claim they were the perogy or Christmas lights capital of Canada. They want those titles, eh. But not the other ones. Seems like no one wants to take too much responsibility for things like youth crime. But anyways, the no name present. Well. I was tryin' to do my best to be more better organized this Christmas. Made a list. Went to check it twice. Found I'd lost the list. So I started over by makin' a list of the lists I needed to make for Christmas. One for presents. One for food to buy. One for Christmas cards to write. On and on, eh. I was thinkin', maybe this gettin' more better organized ain't such a good thing. 'Cause I kine of like runnin' around the malls with that crazed last minute gift buyer look in my eyes, eh. Buyin' whatever's left 'cause the cool gifts have all been bought by the more better organized peoples. Even convincin' myself that just about anybody can wear Brut. I still miss Hai Karate. Maybe they could invent cologne or perfume that men and women could wear. Call it…generic. But anyways, I did do some rearrangin' of the presents under the tree. There's not too many under there, but placement is still important, eh. Bigger gifts to the back and middle of the tree. Little ones out front. And extra special ones, hidden nearby to be revealed at just the right moment, eh. But as I was doin' this rearrangin', I realized there was a no name present under there. I picked it up. Shook it. Even tried to lift the wrappin' where it wasn't taped down. 'Cause I couldn't remember this present, eh. And I didn't want to open it up 'cause I had no more wrappin' paper in the house. I was gonna try steam it open, but what if it was one of those toys that grows 6000 percent when it touches the water? Boy oh boy. I was just stumped, eh. Who was this present for I kept askin' myself. So I sat on the couch and looked at it. Who is this for? And then I thought, kine of strange Christmas predicament. If only I was more better organized and put on a name tag. So. I took a deep breath. An I opened it, eh. And inside…was nothin'. Empty box. And then I remembered what I did. See. The no name present was for me, eh. To remine me. 'Cause I was thinkin' before about this question, "Who is Christmas for?" The kids. Family. Friends. Whoever. But really it's for all of us. You. And me. And that the best presents at Christmas don't come in a box. They can't be wrapped up or be more better organized, but you can still feel them. I wish many blessings on you guys and have a very Merry Christmas. I'm Joe from Winnipeg. Meegwetch.

The Other

Hey you guys, this is me, Joe from Winnipeg. Today I'm gonna be talkin' to you 'bout the other. Happy New Years to you guys. And Happy Millennium. You will be receivin' this message even if there is no radios left runnin' to receive it because of all the power losses due to Y2K bugs, because it was recorded before the turnover. I wanted to do my best to make sure me, Joe from Winnipeg, was Y2K compliant. 'Cept the only thing I could think was recordin' this message ahead of time before all the computers here at the CBC failed and we weren't able to start anything up again. We would've been just like that heritage commercial with the Marconi flyin' kites that have antennas, and only people with Morse code tappers would get this message. 'Cept I wouldn't want to have to be the one transcribin' my English. Ahhh, I'm just kiddin'. Of course I didn't tape this message before the Y2K hit. Seems like that supposed hit felt more like a big fluffy pillow instead of a sledgehammer. You know what I like to believe with all this hysteria that was goin' on? Little bit of fear mongerin'. That so many people was happy and positive and thankful just to be part of histry that that collective will made sure it was all OK. Speakin' of that, oh yeah, the other. That's what I was gonna be talkin' 'bout, eh? Well. I didn't know what else to call it, this idea I got, 'cept maybe the other. I did have another other, but I forgot it. Anyways, the other day I was noticin' how much the other manifests itself in our lives. For some people that was takin' place on New Year's Eve. Wantin' to be at the other party. Or be in the other city. Or the other country. And now we see it with more Y2K warnings. Don't rest easy. It wasn't January 1, 2000. Now it's these other days. And maybe even these other years. And what about all this money the provincial government hasn't been puttin' into the pensions. It wasn't us. It was the other party. Not our government. It was the other government. Boy oh boy, in politics, it's a good thing we got the other otherwise there'd be nobody to hold accountable. And what about the hospitals, "Nope. Sorry. This one's full. Go to that other hospital." That's an old one though, and even most of us when we get sick or something we're always askin' how come it's not the other people it's happenin' to. Instead of us. I guess with all this other business it can seem to be negative, but there's the other other too, eh. The one where we see people sharin' good fortune and helpin' each other. You know, I'm feelin' real good about this Y2K. 'Cause that number 2 that's in there. That's a good reminder to us. 2 us? Hmmm. Even us human bein's are designed for two. There's at least two sides to all of us, two halves to the brain, two lungs, kidneys, feets, hands. Our partner. Opinions. Choices. You name it. So whatever you guys do today, don't forget the other, whatever that may be. I'm Joe from Winnipeg. Meegwetch.

Naught or Aught

Hey you guys, this is me, Joe from Winnipeg. Today I'm gonna be talkin' to you 'bout naught or aught. I'm a little confused about it, so I hope to spread that confusion around a bit by sharin' it with you. Hey. Did you guys check to see if you made the list for the Order of Canada? I hear they give this to Canadians who have made a difference to Canada. They've given out about four thousand of these things. Souns to me like they're about thirty million short there. Awards are funny things. I'm not sayin' don't honour exceptions, but I think all of us Canadians have made a difference to Canada. We are Canada, right? And I know I'm sure a diffrent person now than I was a few years ago. And what's up with this David Crosby and Melissa Ethbridge makin' artificial babies? People can do whatever they want, but I do find it a little bit strange. She says they chose him 'cause of his musical abilities. OK. But I'd want to pay attention to that propensity for alcohol an drug abuse too maybe. Anyways. Naught or aught. First off. Since you can't see the spellin'. I'll spell those words. N. A. U. G. H. T. and A. U. G. H. T. Not, N.O. T. or O. U. G. H. T. 'K? It's kind of funny I'm gettin' a little elementry school here, 'cause that's maybe a good place to start. See. I've been thinkin'. OK. We've been through the fabulous fifties, an the happenin' sixties, an the wacky seventies, an the greedy eighties an the whatever nineties. I'll let you guys put the most appropriate adjective in there for the last decade. But what is this new decade we're movin' into gonna be called? What are all the marketin' and magazine and advertisin' people gonna use for catch phrase, hip, summary adjective? Maybe the elementry or *Sesame Street* Decade 'cause it's gonna be 0, 1, 2, 3, xcetra. This has been confusin' to me. So I looked up the last time it happened, hunerd years ago, an they call that time the 1900's. So maybe this is gonna be the 2000's. But there's somethin' weird about that. Then I thought maybe we could call it the double o's. But in my famly they might be confusin' it with the letter that looks like an upside down "M." The thing I like about the last time we was in this situation was all the excitin' things that happened. Like first airplane flyin'. First Model T. Suffrage movement. Cubism in art world. And the first animated cartoons. Who knows what this decade is gonna bring? Maybe plastic domes over the cities. Whole meals as little pills. Video phones. Flyin' cars. Who knows? Funny thing though, as cool as those ideas soun, all I really hope is that we see less war, more peace. Less human suffrin', more people bein' good to each others. Less despair, more hope. Then I thought how 'bout callin' this decade naught or aught. 'Cause I seem to remember hearin' somewhere that a naught or an aught is a zero. An we've got three of them in this year. I kine of like this name too 'cause with all the excitment that goes with this new millennium we can be reminded about what we ought to do and maybe even what not to do. Hmm. Maybe this decade will be the naughties. I doan know. I'm Joe from Winnipeg. Meegwetch.

The Janitor

Hey you guys, this is me, Joe from Winnipeg. Today I'm gonna be talkin' to you 'bout the Janitor. Boy, oh boy, what's all this business with letters in the news, eh? You got the C R C A C P P R ...uhhh whatever that new party is gonna be called. And how come you can change parties so quickly and even your the principles you're founded on? Who do these guys think they are? Jean Charest. And then even more letters with the IRA. And they're refusing to hand in all their guns. Probably ruinin' that peace deal in Northern Ireland in the process. It always amazes me how people can agree to somethin' and then try to get out of it. Who do these guys think they are? The Canadian government. Speakin' of them, apparently it wasn't a billion dollars that the human resource department wasted on job programs, it was more like nine hunered and niney nine million. It's amazin' what takin' that extra million off the price tag does for the psychology. It just doesn't seem like hardly any money was wasted at all. Anyways, speakin' of waste, I'd better get to what I'm talkin' about today. The Janitor. This has been stuck in my head for the past week now. And I've been thinkin' all about diffrent kines of janitors. The ones we have in our schools. I remember havin' to borrow a mop from the janitor at my school when I was a kid, and I was amazed to see a little cot in his office. His office by the way was full of pipes and old flags and weird stuff like that, kind of made me feel like I was in some special, secret place. But when I realized this janitor took care of that school and even slept there. I got way more respect for him. 'Cause you know, we often don't respect janitors as much as we should. If we even notice them. I know I'm guilty of that myself, except I can't tell if it's 'cause my brother's a janitor or if it's 'cause he's my brother. There's a long line of janitors in my famly. Even me, I was bein' trained to goin' into bein' a janitor, like my father before me, and his father before...no wait, my grampa was a farmer. But I couldn't hack all the stress and co-ordination needed, eh. I remember the anger and disappointment in my father's eyes after I spilled all the dirty water in the mop pail all over the floor. I didn't know you weren't supposed to use your foot to ring out the mop. But anyways, my brother carries on that famly tradition. I asked him what the best part of his job was, and he said, findin' stuff. He works in a government buildin', eh. He tole me he foun a million dollars once, just layin' around. Must be from the human resource department. I'm just kidding, it was really only a pair of running shoes. But they fit. So why all the talk about janitors? Well. The other name for janitors is caretakers, eh. And I met this guy, named Joe, I'm not sure where he's from, but I think it's Winnipeg. And we were talkin' and he ended up mentionin' how all he really wants in life is to be a caretaker. And I was impressed that he wanted to be a janitor. But he said, "No. A caretaker. Of lots of things. My children. Other people's children. Environment. Community. You name it." "Ahhhh," I thought. Not bad. There are so many things we can caretake too, eh. Each other. Ourselves. Federal government's money. We couldn't do any worse a job. So to all the janitors and caretakers in the world: I salute you. Chi meegwetch to yous. I'm Joe from Winnipeg. Meegwetch.

Tap Dancin'

Hey you guys, this is me, Joe from Winnipeg. Today I'm gonna be talkin' to you 'bout tap dancin'. I was gonna be talkin' to you 'bout fare, 'cause I hear the bus fare's goin' up again. I have to laugh 'cause they always used to justify fare increases by sayin' we pay among the lowest fares in the country, but they don't say that no more. And besides, you can argue that just about anything is unfair in some way to somebody, even fares. Hey. Did you guys know that this is the thirty-fifth anniversary of the Canadian flag this week? And that it was first unveiled—Wait a sec. Should that be unflagged? It's not really a veil is it, similar design, but…hmmm. Unfurled maybe. Yeah. Unfurled. Anyways, it was first unfurled right here in Winnipeg. By the then prime minister, Lester B. Pearson. Apparently they heckled him as he was unfurling. Now I don't know what Winnipeggers would've been so impolite, maybe they bused them in from Portage La Prairie. I'm just kidding. I love Portage La Prairieriers. They're some of the politest peoples I know. I just couldn't resist makin' a joke at your expense, 'cause you know Newfoundland's so far away, eh. Anyways, I think the prime minister should be unfurlin' some crisp new hunerd dollar bills here in Winnipeg and Saskatchewan. Help the farmers out. Unfurl maybe 200 million C notes or so. Anyways, what was I…oh yeah. Tap dancin'. Well. I'm talkin' 'bout tap dancin' 'cause that was always a dream my father had, eh. He wanted more than anything to be a tap dancer. I told him, why not be a politician? They tap dance all the time. But he told me metaphors are only useful for understandin', not actually livin'. "You can't live a metaphor, Joe" he'd tell me. And that's true, but it's kind of like…hoa, wait a minute. I better stick to the metaphor at hand here. Tap dancin'. Well, like I said, that was a dream my dad had, eh. Because I understand he was a wicked dancer when he was younger. But he ended up hurting his leg in the war and ended up he couldn't really become a tap dancer, eh. So he became a teacher instead. And many other things too. Anyways, I was talkin' to him the other day, visitin'. And we talked about life and what it can do to you and what you can do with it. And he started talkin' 'bout tap dancin' again. And how he still has that dream. Even though part of me was sayin', but he can't tap dance. But. But. But. Seems like that word always butts in when it shouldn't. 'Cause you know, there's nothing like having dreams. Whatever they are. I hope you guys pursue them. With all the passion and mustard you got. Don't let nobody or no thing get in yer way. Even if people laugh at you or say but, but, but. 'Cause there's nothing as inspiring as seein' someone with hope and dreams, even if we ourselves can't see it, eh. You guys have a good day. I'm Joe from Winnipeg. Meegwetch.

A Beautiful Day

Hey you guys, this is me, Joe from Winnipeg. Today I'm gonna be talkin' to you 'bout a beautiful day. I been hearin' people say lately, "Oh my, what a beautiful day." 'Cause the weather's been so nice lately, eh. All kind of warm, don't really need mitts, and it genrally makes you feel good 'cause you know spring and soon summer will be here, eh. Something nice to look forward to, not like all the gas prices lately. What's up with this? Pretty soon a litre of milk and gasoline is gonna cost the same. That's about where the comparison should end, 'cause one's a bevridge and one's a fuel. I know, I know, milk's a fuel too, but you won't go blind and your kidneys will still function if you drink it. And speakin' of gasoline, boy oh boy, the other day I had to take my friend's car to the service station to fill it up. You notice how that's becomin' an oxymoron too now, "service station," used to be you could get yer tires and oil checked, they'd do your windows for you. Now yer lucky if you even see another human bein' when you buy gasoline. But anyways, this "service station" still had people that wiped yer windows and checked evrything for you. 'Cept I bought my friend's car some gas and waited a long time for the change. (I have to do this for my friend 'cause they're quite environmental and don't want anybody seein' them buyin' somethin' that pollutes the atmosphere.) Anyways, this "service person" doesn't wash my windows. And I got a little bit cheesed off, 'cause one bad side effect of all this beautiful weather is yer windows take a beatin'. Yer constantly usin' that windshield washer fluid, and you can't really seem to be conservative with it neither. You know, save some. 'Cause the car seems to put out at least three squirts regardless. And when you drive a little the car in front of you means you gotta wash the window again right away. And sometimes you try be sneaky and use just the wipers with no windshield washer fluid, but then you get this weird, awful film of dirt. Almost as if the weather knows what yer up to and won't allow it. But thing is, for those of us who live in this part of the country, drivin' with windows that get dirty from beautiful weather, or snow, or they're not defrostin' quick enough and you're drivin' all crouched down lookin' through the part of the window that's defogged, or even doin' the extreme of rollin' down the window and stickin' yer head out to see, all this we're used to it. 'Cause we do what we have to in order to see. Thing is, there's all kines of other things goin' on in this part of the country like people freezin' to death in Saskatoon under suspicious circumstances, or people dyin' here in Winnipeg 'cause they couldn't get help, or any number of these other problems that are plaguin' us here. And some of us aren't tryin' very hard to see. We don't wanna see, eh. Leave that window dirty. If I can't see it, it's not there. Or it's not happenin'. But we know it is. So what are we gonna do? Well, I think givin' that window a good wash and acknowledgin' the problem is a real good first step. The rest of the steps will follow, and then you know what? Oh my, what a beautiful day. I'm Joe from Winnipeg. Meegwetch.

My Eyes

Hey you guys, this is me, Joe from Winnipeg. Today I'm gonna be talkin' to you 'bout my eyes. Kine of the way I see things, but also how my eyes got opened, and I get to see things a little bit diffrently. Sometimes other people sayin' things to me makes this kine of thing happen, like my frien Jeff who was tellin' me horror stories about the big mouse he found in his house, and all the other mouses. It's so bad he doan even like Mickey Mouse no more. I tole him he should get a cat, but then he says, "Nahh. I doan want it to get trapped." An I tole him I didn't know they were trappin' cats these days. Isn't it s'posed to be the mice who is gettin' trapped? But then he says, "No. No. It's that new city by-law thing. Where they trap the cats that are loose." Ohhh. And then I put two and two together, eh. 'Cause I've heard from lots of people in the city that they're havin' mice problems. Homeowners. Business owners. I even heard the post office and some of the shopping malls. And all this mice problems seems to coincide with the cats by-law. People trappin' them. No more cats. Lots more mice. Hmm. And then the big thing that happened to me. I got to go visit the people at Winnipeg Harvest. Now I always thought I knew what the Harvest people did, and even tried to help out how I could. But yet, I never actually visited there before. Let me tell you, it was somethin'. All kines of people. Volunteers. Workers. Friends. Famlies. All of them helpin' to feed other people in some way. There was a big warehouse with all kines of diffrent food and other things to help people, like soap suds and I think I saw little bit of toothpaste. Makes sense, 'cause healthy teeth help chew food. And I saw places where people sit and talk to each others if they're havin' problems, with life, or maybe even ashamed 'cause they have to go to a food bank for the first time. You know, it's funny how society teaches us to feel ashamed if we need help, 'cause there comes a time when evrybody needs help in some way. And there's lots of people who like to help. I even saw this map with all the food banks in the city. There's so many of them. All over. And I talked with David. He's the guy who helps run the Winnipeg Harvest. And he told me all the ways people help them. And it's not just food and money that helps, but time and skills bein' shared. And I noticed that lots of the volunteers and people who helped at Harvest were poor people. And David said, yeah, a lot of people that Harvest helps give back too. Whew. Man oh man. I can't say how powerful this affected me, eh. Really opened my eyes. 'Cause there was all this hard work happenin' to help people, and there was no questioning or people sayin', "If people just weren't so lazy, or worked harder, they wouldn't have to go to food banks." Or all these other excuses we sometimes hear so that we don't have to think about food banks or do anythin' about them, eh. And I'm not askin' you guys to open your hearts or your wallets, but I definitely recommend gettin' yer eyes opened. It's not always pleasant, but it is empowering. And I see what people mean when they say, "I see…" You guys have a good day. I'm Joe from Winnipeg. Meegwetch.

Entertainment Value

Hey you guys, this is me, Joe from Winnipeg. Today I'm gonna be talkin' to you 'bout entertainment value. Did I say that entertaining enough? I hope so. And I hope you get lots more entertainment today than me tryin' to be funny. So I've been noticin' some strange things lately. Like how come we have such a long word to describe places where we can eat? Restaurant. Why not eat? 'Cause you know "restaurant" makes for real long signs. And did you guys hear that some of these beauty pageant contestants may be malnourished. 'Parently their body mass index is lower than the standard set by the World Health Organization. I didn't even know we had a body mass index. I think I prob'ly have a table of contents too. And a title page. And then this other weird thing, these brain doctors are talkin' about our frontal lobes. Apparently if we didn't have frontal lobes we wouldn't have a sense of humour. So that's what's wrong with the prime minister. Hmmm. But anyways, entertainment value. This past weekend I had the pleasure of visiting the beautiful town of Kenora. Now. Apparently Kenora gets its name from amalgamation. Keewatin. Rat Portage and...hmmm. I don't know where the "no" comes from. But I can see why they dropped the "t" off the rat part, 'cause then it would be Kenorat and I think Kenora sounds so much prettier. And boy, is it ever pretty there. It's been so long since I'd been there I'd forgotten. Kind of like how we forget how much we like someone we haven't seen in a long time when we see them again. But I had a real good time in Kenora. Walkin' around. Explorin' the town. Sleeping. Eating. That was real easy 'cause every place had a big sign that said "EAT." Much better than "restaurant." Just kiddin', by the way. And I got to visit too. My good relatives Robert and Jim. That was nice. And real nice when Robert says to me, "Joe, you are good entertainment value." Boy, I've never been a selling point before. And I said, "Well this Kenora's got real entertainment value too. Next time I'm gonna take the extra 5 hours and try out Thunder Bay." 'Cause I found I liked Ontario. No sign of Mike Harris. But I did hear about workfare. So OK, why am I givin' you guys no entertainment value by talkin' about my short holiday weekend? By the way, you're all welcome to come and see all my holiday snaps and if I had videos I'd show you those too. Well. The thing I realized is that we don't have to go far to get good entertainment value, eh. We can find it in our own communities. Or in our own houses and families. Whether that's goin' for a walk or tellin' jokes and stories. And the best part of all, it doesn't have to cost nothin' and it makes ya feel good. Now that's value. I'm Joe from Winnipeg. Meegwetch.

Weather

Hey you guys, this is me, Joe from Winnipeg. Today I'm gonna be talkin' to you 'bout...the weather. (YAWN) Man. What are you guys doin' up so early? Have you guys been spendin' all this time watchin' the Reform Party fill a buster over the Nisga'a treaty? 42 hours or somethin' like that. I mean, I know House of Commons ain't all that intrestin' to watch in the first place, but did they have to do this? And what's up with this stuff anyways? Goin' over this treaty with fine tooth comb, makin' sure all the t's are crossed and all the i's dotted. Comma here and semi-colon there. I hate to say dis, but since when are these guys this intrested in makin' sure a treaty is worded so carefully. I don't seem to recall there even bein' all that much concern about whether the 'Nishnawbe who signed the first treaties could even write. Hmmm. It appears this "x" is incomplete. And by the way, why are all these Indians named "x"? Ahhhh, anyways, I'm sorry to go on a bit there. But I'm so glad to see you guys all here today supportin' Winnipeg Harvest. These guys do good work. And you guys do good work too, by supportin' events like this. And takin' little bit of time to care. So. The weather. Well. Next to food, I guess I talk about the weather the most, eh. And we've sure been havin' weird weather here lately. No snow. Not really too cold. Lots of squirrels runnin' around. I was noticin' some the other day. Yellin' at them, "You guys get to hibernatin'. It's December already." And I was even noticin' the fat little sparrows. They must be mad, eh. "Man here I go get myself all fattened up for a long lean winter, and there's plenty of seeds on the ground. I went and put all this weight on for nothin'." But I hear a lot how the weather's makin' people feel it just ain't Christmas without the cold and the snow. And lots of us have never had a winter like this before, eh. I hear lots of people sayin', "It just ain't quite right somehow." Well, let me talk about news I heard. Big study of homeless people in Nunited States, eh. They find that most homeless people get off the streets if they get some help. Study also supports the idea that homeless people aren't on the streets 'cause of bad choices they've made, but because the government has failed them. Not providin' adequate social assistance and affordable housing. And I think this applies to us here in Canada too, eh. We're taught that these people want to live like that. And it's their fault, eh. But really the government has to take a big piece of that blame. Us too. 'Cause we are our government. Or we should be. They also found out that almost half these people went without food for a day or more 'cause they couldn't afford it. Now here's the thing. You guys have prob'ly heard this kine of thing before, but maybe it might help you to think of the weather a little bit here. You know how some of us haven't been feelin' right this Christmas, like I said before. Well, there's somethin' not right in our community if people have to use food banks more and more, eh. And that's goin' on all the time. Not just at Christmas, but springtime and summer and fall. I really do have to say, from the bottom of my heart, thank yous, 'cause I know lots of people care. And lots of people work hard. Devotin' their whole lives to this problem. I guess, if we use the weather to remine us about things like hunger and poverty, it might help to think that we can't control the weather, eh, but we can rely on it to change. Always changes, eh. And these struggles facin' our community, arson, hunger, homelessness, they can change too. And we control that, eh. I'm Joe from Winnipeg. Meegwetch.

Manitoba

Hey you guys, I'm Joe from Winnipeg. Today I'm gonna talk to you 'bout Manitoba. You know, I got to tell you guys something. I'm really proud to be a Manitoban. I'll tell you why. That election was hard work for lots of peoples, eh. An for some people it turned out the way they wanted. For others not. But I tell you, I haven't been so intrested in seein' how people was gonna vote since the Quebec refrendum. An I really got no comment on how we voted in the end. It was just the fact that we was votin' in the first place. I got real sense of that walkin' aroun the legislature building. I thought, This is great. I belong to this place and it belongs to me. 'Cause see, that word, Manitoba. That comes from Cree word, Manitou. Means Great Spirit. Creator. God. Pretty close too in Saulteaux, Mantou we say. An the idea that Manitoba is the place where the spirit lives, eh. That's good. But you know, I been feelin' this other spirit here too. One that comes from the people that live here. A good feelin'. That we work together an look after our home. This beautiful, rich land, eh. This Manitoba. I'm Joe from Winnipeg. Meegwetch.

Arson

Hey you guys, I'm Joe from Winnipeg. (Holds pot over his head) Boy I haven't done this since we had golf ball size hail, eh. I ran aroun catchin' them to freeze them for later. Why, I doan know. But I wondered why I didn't just do this. Anyways, I was thinkin' about that 'cause of the volcanoes that were eruptin', eh. One in Italy an one in Ecuador. I never seen a volcano, but I'd be pretty scared if I did. The one in Ecuador the 'Nishnawbe there call it "Throat of Fire," eh. Kine of souns like all the people with the flu right now. An the one in Italy, they say the ancient Greek people believed there was a monster under that volcano. Tryin' to escape, eh. Hmm. All this fire makes me think of Winnipeg here a little bit. All the fires we've been havin'. Arson capital of Canada. (Shakes his head) Why? Maybe there's monsters here strugglin' to escape too, eh. Comin' from poverty. Boredom. Stupidity. I doan know. But burnin' things down don't accomplish nothin'. Whoever you might be, if yer watchin' this: Let the fires you set be ones of passion inside you, eh. For your dreams. Your community. That'll warm you like nothin' else. An for the rest of us, maybe we're sittin' on volcano too. One burnin' with anger 'cause of poverty. Bad housin'. You name it. 'Cept diffrence is, dat's a volcano we can stop from eruptin'. I'm Joe from Winnipeg. Meegwetch.

Water Drum

Hey you guys, I'm Joe from Winnipeg. Well. I'm still tryin' to do my best to get ready for this millennium thing. So I'm thinkin' 'bout the future. But not so much our own, but the people that come after us, eh. What kind of world are we leaving for them? I guess what's makin' me think of this is all the news about water. People tryin' to sell water. Half the rivers in the world are dryin' up or too polluted to help us anymore. Emergency outlet for Devil's Lake. Seems to me though, whenever we talk about a solution to these problems, it's technological one, eh. And that's what's gotten us to this situation in the first place. You know, the 'Nishnawbe and all people were given a gift, eh. A gift called a waterdrum. A sacred thing, for our enjoyment and pleasure. It's also somethin' we use to give thanks, eh. It represents many teachings. And all the life in the universe. Thing is, it's called a water drum 'cause you need water in order for it to work. I hope we always have the water drum. And the water too. 'Cause the more we take it for granted, the more we're likely to lose it. I'm Joe from Winnipeg. Meegwetch.

Fuses

Hey you guys, I'm Joe from Winnipeg. Happy New Year 2000. Well. We made it I guess. Although, they keep tellin' us to keep holdin' our breaths. Now it's not January 1, 2000. It's February 29, 2000. And then it's gonna be October 10, 2000. Boy oh boy, I can't tell if all these Y2K experts are like Chicken Littles who keep tellin' us the sky is fallin' or the other ones who keep tellin' us the world is gonna end on such and such a date. Problem with all this stuff is, if we believe it and nothin' happens we're less likely to believe when somethin' really might happen. And look at all the people tryin' to return all the extra bars of soap and generators they bought. No refund, they tell them. I can kine of see that though. "Reason for your return?" "Oh, I, uhh, thought the world was gonna start to end, and since it didn't, I won't be needin' this stuff till maybe February." You know, I never used to know what that meant, "pride before a fall." I thought it had somethin' to do with Shakespeare, but now I think I know. Sort of like "pride before admittin' Y2K was just another year." Thing I find intrestin' about all this Y2K hysteria that some people made lots of money on, boy. And be sure you have a grain of salt for when they tell you it was 'cause they spent all this money preparin' that nothin' happened. 'Cause all the places that couldn't afford to spend any money on their computers, nothin' happened. Human bein's don't like lookin' foolish, but sometimes it's better to take the fall instead of havin' all that pride. 'Cause I like that human bein's make mistakes. How else do we learn anythin'? Right? I know I'm sure gonna be learnin' lots for the rest of my life. I'm Joe from Winnipeg. Meegwetch.

Bitin' the Apple

Hey you guys, I'm Joe from Winnipeg. Today I'm gonna be talkin' to you 'bout bitin' the apple. I know it's s'posed to be bite the bullet. But I says what for? I tink der's been too many peoples tellin' other peoples what to bite lately. Me, I'm gonna stick with apples. How come apples? 'Cause they kine of remine me of fall, eh? An to me, fall means newness. New session of the parliament. New TV season. Back to school. Even da New Year for all our Jewish friens, eh. It's da Rosh Ho shonna. Boy, I gotta say dat slow, so I get it right. I asked my friens what dey do to celebrate dat, eh? Mosely eat, dey tell me. Boy, souns good to me. An. Dey dip an apple in honey, eh. So dat dey'll have a sweet year ahead. Boy, I got a new apple an I got a honey lef over from dippin' my chicken fingers in, eh. Mmmm. I hope all of yous have a sweet year, eh. Maybe we could sen more apples to the MP's, eh? An honey. I'm Joe from Winnipeg. Meegwetch.

Los an Foun

Hey you guys, I'm Joe from Winnipeg. Today I'm gonna be talkin' to you 'bout los an foun. Boy, what's up with poor ole Chretien, eh? That Malaysian guy criticizin' him for not treatin' the "Red Indians" right. I didn't know we was red. I guess dey're gonna have to bring dat colour back in da crayon box. So anyways, my nice mitts dat I was braggin' about. I wen an los dem, eh. I put dem down an den I was walkin' aroun. Boy, pretty soon my hans were gettin' cole an I was thinkin', "Man, it'd be nice to have some mitts. Wait a minute." So here I am lookin' for dem. I doan tink I'd be a very good detective. Dis is da las place I saw dem an dis is da las place I'm lookin'. But you know, lookin' through all dis los, forgotten stuff makes me a bit sad, eh. 'Cause der's all dis other stuff dat people lose an der ain't no box you can go to to fine it, eh. Hope. Faith. Good moods. You name it. Even me. I was gettin' so depressed der watchin' all da bad news. I tink I jus about los my mind. Good ting I got it tied up. So if some of yous los sometin' good, I hope you fine it. Maybe it's in dat person sittin' beside you. Or maybe in yerself. I'm Joe from Winnipeg. Meegwetch.

Hallways

Hey you guys, I'm Joe from Winnipeg. Today I'm gonna be talkin' to you 'bout hallways. I been thinkin' 'bout hallways a lot lately, eh. For two reasons. One 'cause I've been spendin' so much time in dem. And two, 'cause I been seein' people in hallways at the hospital. See. Someone I love very much ended up in the hospital. It's been a hard week. Boy, the hospital experience can be very strange, eh. You do lots of pacing, eh. And when you talk to the doctor it can be almost like you're in a romantic relationship. You listen very carefully to everything they tell you. And you hang on every word. What did they mean when they said that? Does it mean this? Does it mean that? Maybe it means this. You can just go crazy, eh. So after I got tired of pacing in the halls and I had to sit down, eh. And this woman walked by and she said to me, tears in her eyes, eh, "Joe. I don't think you can find much humour here." Know what? She's right. I've been hearin' about der bein' people in hallways in our hospitals. But I didn't know what that meant, eh. Just like lots of our problems we can ignore them if they doan affect us. That's not good. 'Cause sooner or later, most of us end up in a hospital, eh. This whole health care crisis is like a hallway, you know. It's leading somewhere. We just got to make sure it's someplace that's good for all of us. And the people we love. I'm Joe from Winnipeg. Meegwetch.

Bargain Huntin'

Hey you guys, I'm Joe from Winnipeg. Today I'm gonna be talkin' to you 'bout bargain huntin'. Well, that was quite the summer we had, so much happened I can barely remember it. But now it's time to start things fresh, get goin' back to school, get back to work, and even put away some of the lawn furniture and cover up the barbeques. I heard someone sayin' to me that it seemed that this time of year was becomin' a sad time. A time of memorials and rememberin' tragic events. And there's some truth in that eh, but I think it's also a time of renewal for us. And hey, what better symbol of that than puttin' the Golden Boy back on top of the Leg where he belongs? All shiny an new, covered in gold, although I notice there's one part of him that's not covered. Some people even makin' fun of him, but hey, I'd like to see you stand naked in minus thirty-five. See what happens then, eh? Anyways, bargain huntin'. Well, one day I needed to buy myself a brand new fridge, eh. An I decided I was gonna get one of those small ones, but the thing was, I had to work fast, 'cause otherwise all my food was gonna go bad. So I headed out. An right away I found a new little fridge for a real good deal, but I figured, man, if it's this cheap I bet I can find a better bargain somewheres else. So I went lookin' some more, an I looked all over the city, but I didn't find a cheaper little fridge nowheres, eh. So I went back to the first place I was at an tried to buy that fridge, but you know what? It was gone. Sold. My bargain huntin' cost me a bargain. I was so disappointed, an mad at myself too. I got another fridge and I ended up payin' way more than I had to, all because I was bargain huntin'. So. What's up with this Kyoto Accord thing, eh? I'll be honest. I don't know the details of this Accord, all I know is that it's about protectin' the environment, and that Alberta is very upset an the United States won't sign it, and I keep hearin' things like, it's gonna cost too much. We need to know what the cost is to

Canadians before we sign it. We need to be very cautious, blah blah blah. I don't know if this is the absolute best deal for the environment of the world, but at least it's a deal. And if you go bargain huntin' for a new atmosphere, I'll tell you somethin', you're not gonna find another one, eh. It just saddens me that all these people are arguin' about this Accord and nobody's sayin', hey, never mind signin' this or not, this is what our province, our country, our people are gonna do to make the environment better. I hope you guys enjoy all that free fresh air today, 'cause that's one of the best bargains you're gonna find. I'm Joe from Winnipeg. Meegwetch.

Born on the Ocean

Hey you guys, I'm Joe from Winnipeg. Today I'm gonna be talkin' to you 'bout bein' born on the ocean. Bein' born is such a wonderful thing, it's too bad we can't remember it, eh? And then it's too bad there are some things so horrible we can't forget, like what happened one year ago. Except for the innocent people who lost their lives, let us hope that we don't have to remember anything like that ever again. So, did you hear that Switzerland has joined the UN, but yet it is going to keep its policy of neutrality? A tradition going back to the 17th century. OK, but I wonder, is this something to be proud of? Bein' neutral. There was a guy who won a Nobel Prize once, his name was Wiesel an he said a great thing. Neutrality always helps the oppressor. There's nothin' wrong with pickin' sides. Well, bein' born on the ocean. I had this friend whose grandfather was born on the ocean. It was said that he was a man without a country. I guess the equivalent today would be bein' born on a plane. Anyways, I always thought this was kind of cool, bein' born on the ocean. It's a good story an conversation starter. 'Cause all of us like to say where we were born. It's important. It tells us where we come from. Where our roots are. Except I'm startin' to think roots can cause troubles too, like war. You guys must've heard all this talk of war with Iraq? Again. Is the son tryin' to finish off what the father started? Did they leave this Saddam guy in power so they could have someone to fight later on? And why this bad guy? Is it because they know where he is? Aren't there lots of bad guys in the world? Hmmm. I can tell you one thing, I don't want a war. Most people don't. But if we're gonna start actin' like international policemen, why just Iraq? Why not China? Zimbabwe? Iran? I guess I'm confused about this and a lot of things goin' on in the world. But where does it all come from? Maybe it all comes from us belonging to countries. All of the troubles and hatred we see seems to be rooted in where our roots are. I just wonder, if all of us were born on the ocean, would we feel so strongly about goin' to war? Or would we all feel a bit more neutral? I think the oceans are a good lesson to us. 'Cause it's pretty much agreed that nobody owns the oceans. They are what they are. A part of the earth. Yet, we all seem to agree that we can own the land. Strange. I can see how bein' born on the ocean has its advantages, except when it comes to tellin' people where you were born. "Oh, I was born somewhere on the Atlantic." But it could give you a different perspective. Not a neutrality, but a clearer vision. And with all the talk of more war it would be nice to imagine that we all belonged to the same place, the earth, that nobody really owned, and what we all belonged to was something we all wanted to take care of. Not bomb. Or cause death and destruction by flyin' planes into buildings. Or even be inhuman to each other. I'm Joe from Winnipeg. Meegwetch.

Body Language

Hey you guys, I'm Joe from Winnipeg. Today I'm gonna be talkin' to you about body language. Hey, how come evrybody was getting' upset that the GST may go up to 10 percent? Doesn't anyone remember that it was supposed to be nine percent originally? So really, we're only lookin' at a one percent increase. Not three percent. So hopefully that will help lessen the blow, 'cause hey, we got to pay for health care somehow, and don't worry about the fact that people may actually spend less havin' to pay 10 percent in tax. They'll spend the same and projected revenues will be fine and…OK, what can we really do about taxes? Seems to me somebody promised to get rid of the GST, not increase it. But did that stop us from votin' this guy in? Hmmm. Anyways, body language. Well, isn't it amazin' how our bodies can be so expressive, eh? I saw these two guys in traffic the other day an man they were usin' their hands and fingers in ways I never seen before. And then there's the story of how the world's oldest human bein', a woman in Japan, likes to "dance with her hands." Cool. I just wish curlers and guys who shoot pool for a livin' would use more body language. It would just add to the great fun of watchin' these sports on television. I was also wonderin' how come we say that body language is English, 'cause we've all heard that term of puttin' "English" on somethin'. Why not Cree? Or French? Or would this mean an entire new type of body language. What's got me thinkin' about body language? Well, all the posturin' we're seein' goin' on in the world. The governments in the States and Iraq again. Lots of body language goin' on there. And all the unions and health care workers and corporations usin' their body's language to get what they want. And then what about us? Us human bein's who go about our day to day an make the world go 'round, 'cause yeah, really it's us that do that, not money. And what is our body's tellin' us? What language is it sayin'? Eat less fats? Eat more fruits? Don't push yourself so hard. Don't get too stressed out, I need to carry your spirit around for a while longer yet. 'Cause you know, I think our greatest gift as animals is language. It's what makes us human bein's. And whatever language your body is usin' to tell you what to do, please listen to it. It's only gonna tell you what's right and what you need to know. I'm Joe from Winnipeg. Meegwetch.

A Ghost Story

Hey you guys, I'm Joe from Winnipeg. Today I'm gonna be talkin' to you 'bout a ghost story. Well of course it's Halloween, so I thought I'd tell a ghost story today. But I have been noticin' some strange things lately. Like, there's trouble in South Africa and they say it's white extremists or there's problem in the Middle East and they say it's Palestinian extremists and we shake our heads and go, "Hmmm. That sucks," without even realizin' the language. If we say someone's a white extremist or a Palestinian extremist or any kind of extremist, we're really sayin' that their attitudes are possessed by everybody else in their group, right? And they're just the extreme ones, but yet we know this isn't true, 'cause not all Palestinians or "whites" believe that we should hate or hurt other human bein's. Another weird thing I noticed is how candy is a big sign that the world's changed. I was eatin' some love hearts the other day, you know these candies that are real good and you give to someone you got a crush on and they say things like, "chase me" or "you're cute," except now they say things like, "fax me" or "call my cel." What kids are usin' fax machines or cel phones? Ahh well, anyhow, candies… Halloween. Oh yeah, my ghost story. Well OK. Here goes. Once, there was this person and this person lived a pretty good life. They were thankful and happy and lucky. And this person went to work and goofed off sometimes and watched TV and did all sorts of things and even loved listenin' to the radio. And this person helped other peoples and tried to better themselves and read books and newspapers and magazine articles. And the world this person lived in was a place where they could live pretty much without fear, there were bad things goin' on from time to time, but they felt safe. And they would sometimes ask "Man, the world sure is changin'." And that's my little ghost story. I believe in many ways the world we knew and many of us grew up in is gone. It's a ghost now, and more and more we'll talk about what it was like then. And how different things used to be. And I know Halloween's supposed to be a scary time, but you know, I can't find anythin' scarier than turnin' on the news. But…and you know I got to say a "but," even though the world's changed and is changin', I believe we can either let it change as it wants to, or make it change the way we want it to, eh. For the better. You guys have a safe and a happy Halloween. I'm Joe from Winnipeg. Meegwetch.

I Forget

Hey you guys, I'm Joe from Winnipeg. Today I'm gonna be talkin' to you 'bout…uhh…what was I…? Uhm…hmmm…that's never happened before. I forget what I was gonna be talkin' about. But how about those Republicans, eh? Gainin' complete legislative control in the United States, now it should be a lot easier for them to get their agenda passed, not like poor old Jean Chretien, I never knew we could have a lame duck Prime Minister before, but I guess it's happened. 'Cause you know, most of us Canadians expect the Prime Minister is gonna be there for a long time, unless it's Joe Clark. Or John Turner. Or Kim Campbell. And did you guys know that people who eat garlic an onions and scallions are less likely to get some kines of cancer? Brand new study seems to prove this. Hey, my smelly auntie used to eat garlic evry day an claimed it cured her arthritis. I find it funny how once scientists "confirm" somethin', then all of a sudden it's fact. People have known this kine of stuff for years, things like eatin' garlic is good for you, an a little bit of 7up or ginger ale is good for your tummy when it's upset, or what about all the farmers in southern Manitoba usin' WD-40 for their arthritis, hunh? What was I talkin' about again? Boy, you know I've been so forgetful lately, an it's been concernin' me, I even worry that I'm gonna get so forgetful that I won't remember to be worried that I'm becomin' forgetful. I'm not sure if this lack of memory is because I'm part of the Canadian electorate just like everybody else and I can't remember promises like no GST and red books an maybe bein' Canadian itself means bein' forgetful. Maybe it's part of our national identity, eh. You know, other day I was wanderin' around lookin' for my socks that I was gonna wear, an yes they were the same socks I wore the day before, they seemed fine, I did the sniff test on them, anyways, I was walkin' around lookin' for my socks an I couldn't find them an then I looked down, an there they were…on my feet already. I'm not kiddin' you. This happened to me. It's a good thing I don't wear glasses, I'd be wanderin' around lookin' for them an thinkin' it's a good thing I can see, so that I can find my glasses, otherwise… Well, of course I didn't really forget what I was talkin' about today, but isn't it funny how much we can forget these days. You know we just get so busy, an we can forget keys, or to mail letters, or call someone, or even take a minute or two on November 11 to remember. 'Cause you know it's not just another day. It's not a holiday. It's for remembrance. An I really think we're forgettin' that. Me included. An I've been findin' the reason we forget is 'cause we're not focussin' on what's important. I'm Joe from Winnipeg. Meegwetch.

Springrolls

Hey you guys, I'm Joe from Winnipeg. Today I'm gonna be talkin' to you 'bout springrolls. Well it's good to know that all this increased money bein' spent on the border between Canada and the United States is stoppin' all those terrorists, eh? Like guys tryin' to buy gas and people smugglin' cereal and peanut butter. And what's up with this "mastermind" Osama Bin Laden? Makin' more threats an tryin' to scare an enrage people, you know I'm thinkin' more and more that the way to deal with this guy is to stop givin' him a voice. That doesn't mean ignore him, but it does mean stop givin' him a worldwide audience for his hate. So anyways, springrolls. Well, the other day I went to go and buy myself some lunch, eh? And I figured, well one of the benefits of livin' in this beautiful country is that we get a choice of lots of different foods at the food court. So I was thinkin', hmm, what part of the world would it be good to eat from today? An I thought, I know, Asia. That's a pretty big region and lots of diffrent types of food. So I went to this place I always go an I order my rice an chicken an tell them to go easy on the sauce, an this woman who takes my order asks me if I want a springroll with that? An I think, did I want a springroll with that? Is she psychic an somehow knew that I had forgotten part of my order? An then I went, hey, wait a minute, this is a sales technique. This is called upsellin'. She's try to upsell me a springroll, tryin' to make that extra buck. Kind of like you go some places they try to upsell you a pair of socks, or get you to buy photos at their famly photo centre for like 99 cents. So I say, "Pardon?" An she says, "Springroll. You want a springroll with that?" An I think some more an say, "No thanks." "OK," she says, an I feel relieved that I didn't ruin her day by not allowin' her to upsell me that springroll. I guess she figured, on to the next one. An to be honest I don't really debate which part of the world I'm gonna eat from at the food court, I always go for the

138 / JOE FROM WINNIPEG All My Best

Asian food, an that woman always tries to upsell me the springroll. But it gets me thinkin', you know this whole situation with Iraq, that's been goin' on for quite some time now, is the idea of war just an upsell on all of us? Is there another solution? An now that Iraq has agreed to the UN terms what's the U.S. gonna do? Try an find another way to go to war, an don't get me wrong I love Americans, but it seems to me they're really lookin' for a fight. An I even hear some people in the States who want to go to war are sayin' there might be a delay now an the tanks an armies won't get rollin' till spring. I just got this weird feelin' we're gonna be asked for somethin' else now an it's gonna be another upsell, eh, well this version of war isn't quite good enough we need a little extra here. An in a funny way, aren't we bein' asked to believe the same thing over an over, an like that springroll, who's really buyin' it? I'm Joe from Winnipeg. Meegwetch.

Points

Hey you guys, I'm Joe from Winnipeg. Today I'm gonna be talkin' to you 'bout points. Well here's some good news to start the day: One of the banks in Canada is posting record profits. Again. Woo hoo. How come this doesn't make me feel happy? Shouldn't it? You know, maybe it's cause I used to have this feeling that if things were going well with business and the economy that it was good for everybody, but now it just seems like it's good for a few people, not the many. Maybe it's a good time to remember Mr. Spock from *Star Trek*'s words, "The needs of the many outweigh the needs of the few." And boy, do we ever have needs, eh? Hey, I think I mentioned this how that they found that duct tape is good for curing warts, and man, is there anything that stuff can't do? Well, supposedly, now somebody is claimin' that hemorrhoid cream is good for gettin' rid of puffy eyes. Hmmm. Well I don't know about that, but who gets the idea to put this stuff on their face? Anyways, points. Well, the Anglican church and Ottawa have come to some kind of deal about dealing with compensation for those Aboriginal peoples who were abused in residential schools run by the church. And I know a lot of people seem to want this kind of stuff to just disappear and not have to talk about it anymore and... (SIGH) Thing is, there's a way to make that happen, and that's to deal with all these issues, stop arguin' over money and start the healing. But now that Ottawa and the Anglican church have come up with a compensation package, they're not sure how to distribute the money. One suggestion is that they use a point system. You know, you got abused in this way you get so much money, you got abused in that way you get this much money. Sounds like our no fault insurance, you lose a finger you get this much, you lose a leg you get this much. Who comes up with quantifyin' things that don't really have a dollar value this way? So what is the point of all this stuff? Well, to me, the point is it's not about money. That's what all the arguin' and concern is about, but really it's about people. People that were horribly mistreated and now want to heal and get on with their lives, and of course compensation is fair and just, but it can't bring back time lost with families, or learnin' how to be a parent, or a language, or a culture. And the more Aboriginal human bein's are seen as people, the less likely things like this will ever happen. I just felt like pointin' that out. I'm Joe from Winnipeg. Meegwetch.

The Beef or the Chicken

Hey you guys, I'm Joe from Winnipeg. Today I'm gonna be talkin' to you 'bout the beef or the chicken. OK, I find it interestin' what becomes the big story in the news in Canada. Like this aide of the Prime Minister's who calls U.S. President George Bush a moron, and then doesn't really apologize for it. I guess I could say something smart alecky, like "have you looked over your shoulder at your own boss?", but the thing I find interestin' about it, is that there hasn't really been an apology. And now, whatever people think about politicians, me included, we can't forget they're people and it's still rude to go callin' people names right? And why no real apology? Well, as a Native person in this country, I've found apologies have never been easy things for governments or their people to do. And hey, what about all this Miss World, Miss Canada, whatever it is business, that's somehow become a bigger story than the fact that people have died over this so called beauty pageant. Shouldn't a Miss. World be tryin' to make it a better place, instead of appearin' at car shows? Is it just me, or is the world becomin' more frightening? Maybe more absurd. Anyways, the beef or the chicken. Has this ever been like one of the biggest decisions in your life? To have the beef or the chicken, and no offense to the vegetarians, but I didn't want to talk about the fennel or the grain or the soybean, an hey, while I'm on that, how come if people really want to be vegetarians they keep makin' fake meat foods, like soy hot dogs, or veggie meatloaf, or vegetarian-like turkey Christmas dinner? Is that to try an trick the meat eaters you invite over to eat your food? Hmm. Anyways, I often find I have a hard time with choosin' the beef or the chicken. Sometimes it's easy dependin' on mood, or dependin' on whether I've eaten five hamburgers before dinner, but usually I ask for a recommendation, which is strange, 'cause I'm often mistrustful an thinkin', well the waitress is just gonna try push whatever nobody else is eatin'. But regardless, I end up eatin' it anyways. And today's the big day eh. The real big story. 'Cause today's the day that Mr. Romanow has released his big report on health care in Canada. So now the federal, provincial and territorial governments can choose to accept or ignore any of the recommendations in this report. They can take the chicken or the beef, or both, or none. An I do believe there's some real good things in there. An thankfully I doan have to ask, "Where's the beef?" An I'm hopin' our governments won't be chicken an will make the hard choices. The ones that can cost them their jobs, but will end up makin' our nation an our people stronger. An healthier, 'cause you know whenever I hear people arguin' over who or what is a Canadian, I just look at our health care system an our obsession with it. Canadians are people who want to be healthy, that's why we live in such a great country. I'm Joe from Winnipeg. Meegwetch.

A Drop in the Bucket

Hey you guys, I'm Joe from Winnipeg. Today I'm gonna be talkin' to you about a drop in the bucket. So did you hear that the Snowbirds may have to wait until 2020 to get new planes? That's like eighteen years. That's an outrage. 'Cause you know the Canadian military is really good at bein' in parades an airshows. So, they should make this a fundin' priority, eh. I know our military's budget is like peanuts, an we always expect the U.S. to look after us, but we could be puttin' those few peanuts we got left to good use, eh. Hey, I got to just throw somethin' out here, you know, the other day I happen to catch this guy blowin' his nose, I wasn't watchin' him or anythin', it just kind of happened, anyhow, he blows his nose into a piece of Kleenex, an then…an then, he unwraps the piece of used tissue an looks at what he just blew out of his nose. Is this normal? Are there two types of people in the world? The kind who use Kleenex for what it is and throw it away and the kind who use tissue an then check to see what they left behind? If so, what kind am I? What kind are you? Hmmm. Anyways, a drop in the bucket. Well, how many drops does it take to fill up a bucket? A lot, eh. Sure. But we're not really sure how many, we just know it's a lot. An how big of a bucket are we talkin' about? That's important too. Well, I just been hearin' how the Auditor General of Canada is wantin' some answers. Like how come this gun registry thing is costin' at least a billion bucks. Only nine hundred ninety seven million dollars more than they said it was gonna cost. Or why does the E.I. system have a surplus of 40 billion dollars? Or even that First Nations are bein' made to spend some of our precious few bucks on reports that don't even get used or read. Man, we're talkin' about a lot of drops in the bucket. And now we're bein' told that E.I. premiums will drop 10 cents. Wow. Really? Hey man, now I can get that piece of Bazooka Joe bubblegum I wanted for Christmas. So all this may seem like more grousin' an nothin' ever changes an what can we do about it all? Well, if all those drops in the bucket are our money we should be doin' somethin' about it. If you were overcharged 40 billion bucks at the store you'd say somethin' about it. Right? 'Cause I think a lot of us forget that all that tax money is our money. An I think the more we look at it that way, the less likely we're gonna be just goin' through all that money like water. Pourin' it down the drain. Lettin' it be lost like tears in the rain. OK, I'll stop now. I'm Joe from Winnipeg. Meegwetch.

Syndromes

Hey you guys, I'm Joe from Winnipeg. Today I'm gonna be talkin' to you about syndromes. So'd you hear about this woman who fell asleep on the plane and ended up getting' like 15,000 air miles 'cause she ended up in England instead of Newfounland? Man, I wish that happened to me evrytime I fell asleep on the bus, I wouldn't have to worry about buyin' a ticket again. It is kind of a tough one, 'cause I think it's kind of nice that they let her sleep, but at the same time, don't you think they should've known she was only goin' so far? Maybe this would be a nice way to get to Vancouver, buy your ticket to Regina an then pretend you fall asleep an wake up in Vancouver. So anyways, syndromes. Well, what's got me goin' on about syndromes is that I was hearin' about this thing called Hurried Woman Syndrome. And it afflicts women who are livin' modern lives an takin' care of their kids and their families and cookin' the meals and drivin' kids to lessons and practices and tryin' to take care of themselves an all that stuff and whew. Well, now there's a name for it. Hurried Woman Syndrome, and it has symptoms like weight gain, getting' tired, bein' moody. Hmmm. Sounds like other things to me, but the guy who's invented this. Or givin' it a name has a new book out. It's called Hurried Woman Syndrome and… OK. Now I'm not sayin' that people don't have afflictions and things, eh, but since when did all these diseases and afflictions and intolerances become big business. When I was growin' up, there was no such thing as lactose intolerance. Or severe allergies. Or Hurried Woman Syndrome or Chronic Fatigue Syndrome, now I'm not sayin' by any means that these things aren't real, but do you guys think it's possible for a minute that somebody's makin' money off of all this? Sellin' books. Sellin' special kind of milks. Medications. And, and, if these things didn't exist before and are now very widespread, what's that sayin' about our environment and the way we live our lives, I think it means somethin' is makin' us sick. And that's not good. I just really am confused, and yes, I'll admit a little suspicious about all this, 'cause who's to stop anybody from comin' up with a syndrome. Hey mom, I can't go to school, I've got Lazy Kid Syndrome. Your kid doesn't want to get up and go to school? Wants to watch TV and play video games all the time? Eat junkfood? They may have Lazy Kid Syndrome. Are you lookin' for a deal all the time? Do you talk about the weather lots? Are you a bad driver? You may have Winnipeg Syndrome. Where does it end? An what about all the for real syndromes that need our attention? Will they get less because of this? Just make sure you don't find yourself catchin' some kind of syndrome, eh. Be as healthy as you can an don't get the syndrome of havin' a syndrome, eh. I'm Joe from Winnipeg. Meegwetch.

A Black Guy, a Jew and an Indian

Hey you guys, I'm Joe from Winnipeg. Today I'm gonna be talkin' to you about a black guy, a Jew and an Indian. Now don't get offended, I aim to be not even the least bit offensive an I'm going to fully explain an rationalize what I'm talkin' about today. OK? Hey, you know what? I think the world is really endin'. Why? Well, for the first time in its history, McDonald's is gonna suffer a loss in its earnings. First time ever, in like almost fifty years. Is this not a sign the world is endin'? An maybe that's good, maybe somethin' healthier and new is startin'. Anyways, a black guy, a Jew and an Indian. Well, the reason why I'm talkin' about this is that I always wondered how come someone didn't make a joke about this. Now lots of people right away say that isn't funny, an that only someone who was of African Canadian or Jewish or Aboriginal heritage could tell it, but what would that joke be about? How dare someone tell it? How dare someone suggest it, eh? And what's got me talkin' about this? Well, with the remarks made by Mr. Ahenakew and Mr. Lott in the States, both sayin' some things that they say they're sorry for an that were taken out of context an that they needed to rationalize an explain an that got people really upset. Well…I do find it interestin' that both these guys are older men. I also find it interestin' that some people are feelin' the apologies are not enough. Hmmm. What's a good alternative? Get inside them an change how they think? That prob'ly would be best, but not very ethical or possible. An focusin' on Mr. Ahenakew for a second, I find it interestin' how much attention this story is gettin'. An now, NOW I'm not justifyin' what this man said in anyway, but things just as wrong have been said by lots of other people and I've noticed it hasn't gotten the same amount of attention. Is it because people won't stand for this kind of thing at all anymore? Maybe. Maybe the world is endin'. Or is it because of somethin' else. An that's what I think. 'Cause I think part of it is that Mr. Ahenakew is an Indian. An lots of people still think Indians can't, that's CAN'T, say things like this. Why? Well, Indians, if they're not street people, are wise an tolerant an in harmony with nature. If only that were true, but instead, Indians can be just as stupid an prejudiced an hurtful as anybody else. An if it's so shockin' to people that someone of Aboriginal descent can speak some hate, maybe it's 'cause we're still not bein' seen completely as human bein's. An as for that joke about the black guy, the Jew an the Indian, well, I think it would be about comparative sufferin'. Who's suffered the most. Well, the children of Africa 'cause they were slaves an all the horrible things that happened to them, no, no the children of Israel 'cause they were slaves an all the horrible things that happened to them, no, no the Indians 'cause…you see where this is goin'? It's not really the point. Seems the point is we're always gonna have people sayin' stupid, hateful things, an inappropriate jokes, an strong reactions until this world ends. An a new one starts, eh. One where jokes start with…there are three people an there's no language to create hate an everyone's seen as a human bein'. I'm Joe from Winnipeg. Meegwetch.

Pasta Pot

Hey you guys, I'm Joe from Winnipeg. Today I'm gonna be talkin' to you about a pasta pot. Did you guys hear that there's a new book out stirrin' up all kines of controversy. It's called *1421: The Year China Discovered America*. I guess some people don't like the idea that it wasn't Europeans who "discovered" America. It was the Chinese who "discovered" America. That's funny, I didn't know that Native peoples and their lands were "discovered"? You know what really bugs me, is that people still go around thinking this land was "discovered." And the assumption that what existed here before was "primitive," hey it wasn't perfect, but it sure couldn't have led to anything worse than we got now. And what's up with bein' the premier of B.C.? Does takin' this job mean you have to mess up somehow? Thinkin' of endin' that political career? Become premier of B.C. Seems like these guys spend more time in a court room than in office. And I don't know, man, but he prob'ly shouldn't have been smilin' in that one picture they took of him. And people seem to be 50-50, eh, some say he should resign, some say forgive him, I doan know, I just know havin' around 50-50 support is only good enough if you're havin' a referendum in Quebec. So, anyways, a pasta pot. Well, OK. I got to sound off about these things. I see this commercial for a pasta pot, an when they show people tryin' to cook pasta the "regular" way, all of a sudden they become two-year-olds. Don't you just hate it when this happens to you? And you see someone dumping pasta into the sink. And the family's at the table really upset 'cause their dinner isn't ready, thanks to silly old mommy, who didn't have the pasta pot. And what about all the other commercials like this? Don't you just hate it when your garden hose gets all tangled up. Stop! Try this new hose that your car can drive over. Got a dent in your car? Use this. It's what professionals use. Uhhh no. Sorry. Professionals don't use chunks of plastic that cost $12.95. And on and on. Now don't you think if these things were as revolutionary and as great as they say they were we'd all have Popeet and Ginsu knives in our kitchen? And shredding twirly things that let us make radish flowers and twirly potatoes? And none of our in-laws would ever come back 'cause we'd be slicing meat so thinly and evrybody would be readin' the newspaper through a tomato. But instead what's happened? We're using what we've always used. And what works. And how come we keep hearin' the same song and dance out of George W.? He's sick and tired of games and deception. Whose games and deception? Maybe he's waiting for evrybody to go, "OK, that's it. Just bomb them already. Go to war. That's what you want right?" I just think this new showdown with Iraq is old and tired an if you want somethin' new an improved, go to what's always worked in the past. And then maybe the world can focus on the challenges that really matter, like our environment, people suffrin', and peace. OK, I'm gonna go try an figure out how to make my Christmas present of a curly hair spinning twisty thing work. I'm Joe from Winnipeg. Meegwetch.

The Woodpile

Hey you guys, I'm Joe from Winnipeg. Today I'm gonna be talkin' 'bout the woodpile. Boy there's some strange stories goin' around out there. Did you hear this one about this guy who had his head reattached? For real. I guess he was in an accident and they had to put his head back on and now it's working again. I guess there's lots of women out there who don't think this would be a bad idea for most men, eh. An then they asked people what the most important invention is, what they absolutely cannot do without. Computer? Nope. Car? Nope. TV? Nope. Bannock? Nope. Well, that's what I would say, but they say toothbrush. Isn't that somethin'? I had no idea people were so into dental hygiene, from the look of some people's teeth that seems a bit surprising. And you know what my brother used to say, he'd say, you know it's Indians who invented the toothbrush and the toothpick, 'cause if it was anyone else they'd call them teethbrushes and teethpicks. He also used to say this joke, "How do you compliment an Indian?" I doan know, I'd say. "Nice tooth." And then he'd laugh an flash his tooth at me. Anyways, the woodpile. Well, census numbers are out and they're sayin' that Winnipeg has got more Indian people in it than anywhere else. Like 55,000 of us. And that's just the people who'll admit it. 'Cause you know it's not so long ago, and even today that some people who were Native wouldn't admit it. But that's changin' as we find pride in ourselves and who we are. Other thing this census says is that we now have more immigrants than we've had since the thirties. And that almost twenty percent of the people born in Canada were born somewheres else. Wow. A big challenge, 'cause it means that the fabric of this country, which is its people, is gettin' rewoven. And that means that the way we view ourselves as Canadians is gonna have to change. You know, I knew this guy who used to always say that all the people in Canada have somethin' in the family woodpile they don't talk about, or don't want to admit. I used to hear that about Native people and families, 'cause you know, it is hard to find someone who's third generation Canadian who doesn't have Aboriginals in their woodpile, eh. I guess with Canadian woodpiles changin' though maybe it's finally time for Canada to reconcile itself with its past and its future. For real. 'Cause you know havin' a rich woodpile is a wonderful thing. It keeps ya warm. It rests easy against the side of the house, maybe even supports it a little. And it's heritage. Somethin' you can brag about. I'm Joe from Winnipeg. Meegwetch.

Senior Moment

Hey you guys, I'm Joe from Winnipeg. Today I'm gonna be talkin' to you 'bout…uhhh…what was I? Hmmmm. Anyways, you guys hear about one of these bankers makin' over five million bucks for his salary? How does that work, I wonder? Like…your pay would be…almost a hunerd thousand dollars a week. What would your EI and CPP deductions be? Would you be like…man forty-six thousan dollars? This government's killin' me. I gotta move to a tax haven like the Cayman Islands or Alberta. So…what was I gonna be talkin' about today? Did I say that yet? I…oh yeah, today I'm gonna be talkin' to you about a senior moment. Yeah. That's it. A senior moment. Hey, how come people don't do the macarena anymore? You know what I think's even weirder that people don't do it anymore, is that some people actually remember how to do it? And I'm not sure about this, but did the macarena come along before line dancin' or after? Maybe it was responsible for creatin' the line dancin' craze. And speakin' of that, do people still line dance? I mean I got to admit I don't go to too many cowboy bars 'cause I'm an Indian. Not sayin' I wouldn't be welcome, but it would kind of be like Jack Layton walkin' into the House of Commons and sittin' down. Don't you think the other MP's would start whisperin' an sayin', "Is he supposed to be here?" "He's not elected, is he?" "Who invited him?" Anyways, what was I…hmmm…oh yeah, a senior moment. Well, I was at this great event with lots of wonderful peoples and they were celebratin' family an good things like that an speeches were bein' made an all kines of other cool stuff an then somebody stood up an was givin' a speech and…and…oh yeah, and they kept forgettin' where they were an then finally said, well I keep havin' this senior moment. Actually, they had several senior moments, but could only remember the last one. And you know it's not only seniors who have senior moments. Look at the President

154 / JOE FROM WINNIPEG All My Best

of the United States. Preparin' us for war. Man, if this guy took as much care preparin' his country for social reform, imagine how much greater a place the States would be. An is Jean Chretien havin' senior moments more often? He is a senior, right? An why is it that we readily accept seniors as politicians but in very few other jobs? Hmmm. I think the best senior moments are the ones we make ourselves, when we hook up with the elders in our lives, and let them know they're appreciated and loved. I'm Joe from Winnipeg. Meegwetch.

Three Cents

Hey you guys, I'm Joe from Winnipeg. Today I'm gonna be talkin' to you about three cents. So. Well. Hmmm. Wow. What a difference a week makes, hunh? Lots has changed in the world already. Did you know that yesterday was the 100th anniversary of the Wright Brothers' flight? 100 years. And look at us now. We're flyin' all over the place. To other communities. Other countries. Even the moon. I'm not quite sure if all this flyin' has made the world seem smaller or bigger. Anyways, poker. Well, let me tell you a story, when I was a kid, about 10 years old, I was playin' poker with my cousin. And we decided this was gonna be a real serious game with all the change we had in our pockets. So we laid all our copper and silver on the table there and we had real impressive little piles of money. I had a little over 60 cents, my cousin, just under 70 cents. Anyways we get playin' this game and after a while my cousin starts braggin' that he has won more money from me than I have from him. And we start yellin' at each other eh. Boy, it got so serious my auntie said, "You boys. Cut that out. Count how much money you have and settle your argument." Good idea, we thought. So we counted our money and turns out my cousin had about three cents more than me. And we were kind of shocked, dismayed, and then we laughed about it. But I tell this story 'cause I find it funny how much arguin' we can get into over a little bit of money. And what's with poker anyhow, we shouldn't have been playin' it. The game's always seemed a little "dirty" to me somehow. And lookin' at what's goin' on in the world right now leaves me scratchin' my head. Our new Prime Minister is arguin' about how Canada should be allowed in on the contracts to rebuild Iraq. Ohhh, I see, so we put sanctions and bombed that country so that we could make money rebuildin' it. And now that they've caught Saddam Hussein, who they somehow managed to make some people feel sorry for despite all the bad things he's done, and now that they've caught him they're askin' the President of the United States if he should be executed. Well that's a bit like askin' me if I'd like to have some more butter tarts after I've already eaten five. Of course I'll have more 'cause I love them. George W. Bush signed the execution order on hundreds of people while he was Governor of Texas, it's not like he's all of a sudden gonna be lenient. And you know what really bugs me about all this? About all of our current world leaders, it feels a bit like that poker game and the three cents. We're arguin' over money. Not the real important stuff, like the people of Iraq, or the soldiers who are fightin' a war 'cause they're ordered to. And it all feels slightly dirty. Pick any one of these guys. Saddam Hussein. George Bush. Tony Blair. Ariel Sharon. Paul Martin. One's a mass murderer. One's started a war. One's lied. One hasn't kept a promise they made. One's involved in a money scandal. One's usurped the leadership of his country. And these are the guys we're supposed to trust? They speak about truth, justice and loyalty, and yet don't seem to demonstrate it in their own leadership. I don't know. I think when the dust settles from all the upheaval the world's going through we'll find the values we cherish most as human bein's will be better expressed in our leaders. I'm Joe from Winnipeg. Meegwetch.

The Flood of the Century

Hey you guys, I'm Joe from Winnipeg. Today I'm gonna be talkin' to you 'bout the flood of the century. Wow. Christmas is almost here, eh? That's pretty cool. But I been hearin' how some of you guys don't got the Christmas spirit. Wait a second, did I just use a double negative? "Don't got," nope, I'm OK, just bad use of English. There's way too much negative goin' on already anyhow. But if you don't "have" the Christmas spirit, have I got a solution for you. Shoppin'. Get out there and buy buy buy. Spend money and get presents for people. Yourself included. What's that? You don't got no money? Well, that's what credit's for. Goin' into debt so that you can buy stuff. And…wait a second, what am I sayin'? I think I was bein' possessed by the bad Christmas spirit of consumerism there for a second. Now I'm not anti-consumerism, we need trade, but when that's gettin' used to replace the real Christmas spirit it ticks me off a bit. Speakin' of anti stuff, did you guys know that my cousin was anti auntie? That's right, and I'm not talkin' a double negative here neither. See, he didn't like how my one auntie always made him kiss her for a dollar. He tried to tell me she had a bit of whiskers and it burnt his face when she kissed him, but I told him he was just makin' excuses, bein' all anti auntie. Which isn't good neither, 'cause we should love our family, especially the ones with whiskers. Well, to make a short story long, turns out he escaped those dollar store kisses from my auntie by gettin' her to focus her attention on me. And I got to say, I'm workin' hard not to be anti auntie. Anyways, the flood of the century. Well, we had that here in Manitoba last century, eh? Last millennium even. Oh, that was tryin' times for people. Everybody was stressed out and communities were threatened and it was just generally crazy. But you know what happened durin' those rough times, was people in Manitoba came together. Put aside prejudices and differences of opinion and worked towards a common good. Man I liked that. And the other day I was walkin' through a mall and not feelin' terribly Christmassy, when I see this older man with his familiy, and then I saw some more families and then I saw people shoppin' and buyin' lottery tickets and sittin' on Santa's lap, and then Christmas got really big for me. It flooded over me. And I realized that all over the world people are doin' this same thing. Gettin' ready to celebrate this ritual time that's lost its meaning for many people, but it's still understood that this season is about family and love, peace and good will towards all people. And I took great comfort in that, that during the times that try us we should remember we're not alone. There's a great flood of humanity that feels the same way you do, and does the same things you do, all over the world. And many of them believe in that same spirit of the holidays that we all want to see flood over the world. Peace. Love. Good will to all people. Merry Christmas, you guys. I'm Joe from Winnipeg. Meegwetch.

Covergirl

Hey you guys, I'm Joe from Winnipeg. Today I'm gonna be talkin'
to you about covergirl. I was goin' down Main Street the other
night, the snow was fallin' and I was lookin' at some Native-run
businesses and thinkin', man Native people, we've come so far, and
yet…we have so far to go, as I watched the police trying to arrest a
Native guy. But I guess with all the good there's always gonna be
some bad. Speakin' of that, you guys hear that another Canadian
spy plane crashed? That makes four of them out of commission,
which I guess is all of them. Canadian spy planes? Is it just me or
does the concept of that seem strange, kind of like saying Canadian
nuclear arsenal? I'll leave the good and bad up to you. Anyways,
covergirl. Well I was watchin' the TV the other day and there was
this ad that came on. And it was for Covergirl. I think that's some
kind of makeup, Queen Latifah was talkin' about having longer,
thicker eyelashes. Which I don't have to worry about 'cause mine
are already long and thick, in fact they tickle my cheek evry time I
blink. And how do you get the name "Queen," not a title, do you just
make it up? From now on I'm gonna be Queen Stronach, which I'm
not sure if that sounds better than Queen Belinda or not. 'Cause you
know if that's the case we could all be kings and queens. Anyhow,
as I'm watchin' this so many things are swirlin' around in my head.
Things like President George Bush's State of the Union address, and
how this man got "elected" to office in the first place. Or did he
really? And yes, terrorism is a big threat in the world, but does that
mean we start a war against whoever? Doesn't seem as right as he
tells us. And the story that some police officers at the Ipperwash
standoff were saying prejudiced things before Dudley George got
shot. Or the conditional sentence given to this guy who attacked
someone he thought was someone else, like that's somehow an
excuse for that behaviour. A lot of it just doesn't seem fair. And this

troubles many of us because we've always been taught to play fair, or be fair in all that we do. Which flies in the faces of how life actually seems to be. I guess it's kind of like the covergirls. To some of us it isn't fair that there are human bein's who most of us agree look more attractive than a lot of us. Why's that? How come so many of us don't already have perfect lashes? Why can't I fit into a size six? So how do we cope? Well, we accept it. We accept that this is how things are, or this is what has happened, no matter how unfair it is. 'Cause life will always have unfairness in it. But it's what we do after that that becomes important. Do we shrug our shoulders and say, OK, I'm fine with that, or the way things are. Or do we do somethin' positive about it, in whatever form that takes, speaking up or maybe even creating a new standard of beauty with short, cute eyelashes? I'm Joe from Winnipeg. Meegwetch.

Right

Hey you guys, I'm Joe from Winnipeg. Today I'm gonna be talkin' to you about right. Boy oh boy, tough time to be head of a Crown Corporation, eh? Seems you get suspended for some reason or another. But somehow that doesn't seem that bad, it sounds kind of like what they did to the semi-bad kids at school. They suspended them. If you were really bad you got expelled. Maybe that's what happens next. And how come nothing seems to be happening to the politicians? And I know this might not be too popular, but you know of all that money that got spent, some of it actually did some good. Anyways, right. Well some strange goin's on. I hear the President of the United States wants to make an amendment to their constitution banning gay marriages. Whatever happened to live and let live? And I keep hearin' how this is a threat to the institution of marriage. Hunh? Some say it's being redefined. Maybe a little, but isn't it still about two people loving each other and making a commitment? But then this is a country which has an amendment to its constitution that gives its citizens the right to bear arms. And hey, Mel Gibson's new movie about Mel Gibson is out I hear. Lots of people gettin' upset about it, but didn't Jesus tell people to love your neighbour as you'd love yourself? And not to judge anyone or else you might be judged? He didn't say, well, you can judge gay people for their behaviour, but not anybody else. Behaviour. Listen to me. I'm startin' to sound like them. Whoever they are. And speakin' of right, you ever wonder why right wing and the right have adopted that name? And the other side, the left side, the one that's historically considered the bad side to be on, is left bein' called the left? Hmmm. But the thing that's got me thinkin' about right is downloadin' music. I know lots of people do it. OK, millions of people do it. And I'm hearin' corporations sayin' what you're doin' is wrong. It's not right. It's theft. And then the people who download say, they make billions anyways, and they've been rippin' us off for years, so who cares. It's my right to download music. Which as an interestin' side note, if I bought a CD and lent it to twenty people, is that illegal? Kinda seems the same to me. But OK. OK, no choosin' sides here, but the thing I figured out about who's right and who's wrong is, don't you think that if all these companies that make money off of sellin' music and movies and whatever else is bein' "illegally" downloaded and stolen or whatever you want to call it, don't you think that if they gave back more of the money they took out of people's hands and our communities, that people would want to see those companies thrive? They'd want them to be successful and not risk goin' out of business. Instead, what's happenin'? Most people don't care. 'Cause as human bein's we believe that what's really right is a sense of fairness. Even sharing. I think some of those Liberals figured that out, although they shared in the wrong way with maybe the wrong people. So as for what's right? I think helpin' the great communities we all live in, whether they're local or global, is right. I think livin' and let livin' is right. And I guess if I was in a relationship my partner would always be right. Good advice. I'm Joe from Winnipeg. Meegwetch.

An Expensive Shot

Hey you guys, I'm Joe from Winnipeg. Today I'm gonna be talkin' to you 'bout an expensive shot. Boy oh boy, what kind of craziness goin' on among us human bein's. You guys hear about this woman who tried to use a million dollar bill at Wal-Mart? You got to admire those kind of guts on some level, but the sad thing is, who knows, in a few years we may all be usin' million dollar bills instead of twenties. Maybe she thought she was in Japan or Italy? And Sheila? Good heavens, this thing is starting to sound like some of the nominations and elections on reserves I've been to. RCMP bein' called. Charges of fraud and supporters bein' kept off of lists. It's crazy. The one thing I learned is that in politics, rock 'n roll and acting, if you stick around long enough you've always got a good chance for a comeback. Anyways, an expensive shot. Well, I was in a strange mood the other day, as I'm walkin' downtown and missin' Eaton's and seein' this new arena goin' up in Winnipeg, I guess I was feelin' nostalgic. Even missin' the Winnipeg Jets. And thinkin', well it was nice when we had them, but I guess we couldn't really afford them and things seem to have changed in hockey and then I thought, well yeah, I guess things have changed, but some things haven't. Like this guy named McSorley takin' a swing at someone's head with his stick, and a guy named Cicarelli who did the same thing, and now we got some guy breakin' some other guy's neck by givin' him a cheap shot. Excuse me? Cheap shot? So if there's a cheap shot, which is obviously unacceptable, then I guess there's an expensive one as well. Which I guess would be OK, which must be when one hockey player comes up to another one and says, "OK, man, I'm going to physically attack you now. And give you an expensive shot. 'Cause you know, I don't believe in cheap ones." Why do we accept this? And they call this a game? And speakin' of expensive shots, why are some people tryin' real hard to bring an

NHL team back to Winnipeg? So we can give out huge tax breaks and regain our profile in North America? Good idea, 'cause I hear Columbus, Ohio is world famous now. Don't mind me, I'm just not all that crazy about the guy that city's named after. And since I'm goin' on about expensive things and bringin' a hockey team to Winnipeg to help our community, isn't Manitoba still the child poverty capital of Canada? Oh, I'm sorry, I guess that was a cheap shot. But hey, you guys have a good day. I'm Joe from Winnipeg. Meegwetch.

Missin' Index

Hey you guys, I'm Joe from Winnipeg. Today I'm gonna be talkin' to you 'bout a missin' index. Sounds kind of financial or somethin', eh? Ahh, don't worry, it's kind of grosser than that. Hey, how come we always have to wait while the bus driver stops the bus and runs in to buy a donut, and yet he never waits for us when we're runnin' to catch the bus? Maybe they're in a hurry to buy donuts. Anyways, a missin' index. Well, I had to go to the funeral of my Auntie Beatrice this week. She was 98 years old. And what a wonderful woman she was, she helped raise me and she was full of faith, eh? Anyways, while I attended her funeral in one of my homes, Kinosota, 'cause see I feel I have many homes in Manitoba, and Kinosota is one of my favrits, anyways, while I was there I hooked up with many people I hadn't seen in many years. And it was so nice that I got to connect with old friends and family members, but sad that this was the occasion it was happenin' on. And while I was visitin' there I got talkin' to my auntie's brother, Charlie. And he said to me, Joe, I'll never forget my sister. And I said, me neither. I loved her. Many people did. Me too, he said, then he told me a story. He said, I always used to joke with her that I wouldn't forget her 'cause of this. And he showed me his hand, and he was missin' his index finger, eh. He said, when he was a baby he was crawlin' behind his sister Beatrice while she was puttin' wood in the stove, and his mom said, watch out for the baby. And Auntie Beatrice stepped back so that she wouldn't do that and accidentally stepped on my finger, with a wide oxford heel, kind of like the women used to wear. And it crushed my finger, Charlie said, and he finally got it removed when he got married. Maybe Charlie was tryin' to save some money on a ring, I'm just kiddin'. But there was no bad feelings in the story, just somethin' bittersweet, which was how lots of us felt. Glad that she lived a long life, but sad that she was gone. And I was thinkin', I'm glad I didn't have to lose a finger to have stories about my auntie, but this missin' index made me think about how some of us are missin' a different kind of index. 'Cause I know an index in a book helps us find what we're lookin' for. You pick up the latest book on say, Elizabeth Taylor and you can look up "husbands" right away, might be half the book, but you can find it easy. But seems so many of us are missin' that index that helps us find solutions to problems we run into. Maybe it's someone mistreating us. Maybe feeling lonely. Maybe just lookin' for some advice. And where is our index? Well, it's there, actually. In our family. Our friends. All kinds of people we love. But somehow we seem to be reluctant to look up some help. I'm not really sure why that is, but it's easy to fix. So I hope you guys make some time for yourself this week, and get pointed back in the right direction if you need it. I'm Joe from Winnipeg. Meegwetch.

Indian Givers

Hey you guys, I'm Joe from Winnipeg. Today I'm gonna be talkin' to you 'bout Indian givers. I know, I know, it's not considered a very "correct" or polite term, but I'll do my best not to be offensive. Although, I'm finding that no matter what I do can be seen to be offensive by somebody. Hey Joe, you're wearin' dead animal skins. That offends me. Hey Joe, you talk weird. I'm offended. Oh well. I just wondered when we all became so intolerant of each other. Maybe we always were, and now we just feel we have the right to be rude. Anyways, Indian givers. Well, there are some interesting origins on this term. But basically we all know what it means, that it's somebody who gives a gift and then wants it back. How rude is that? I know there are some people who wish they had so-called Indian givers giving them presents. Oh, you gave me socks, and a macrame plant holder thing. What's that? You want it back? Oh, OK. No problem. And what's got me thinkin' about the term Indian giver? Well, this thing about pictures and the Beaverbrook Gallery in New Brunswick. Apparently the grandchildren of this guy who gave these valuable paintings to this gallery want those pictures back so they can sell them. And now there's a big fight over it. It's gotten so nasty. And I'm thinkin', why are people goin' so crazy, I mean it's good that art is valued so much, but what's at the heart of this dispute? Ownership. And beyond that, money. So let's look at at that term Indian giver again. Now there's actually some truth in Native people taking back gifts. Why would they do that? Were my ancestors bein' rude? Not at all. It's just that if you have no idea or belief in the concept of money you gave people gifts and in return expected one of equal value. So if you didn't receive that you took your gift back. Makes sense to me. And you know what makes even more sense to me. Gettin' rid of money. I know that's not gonna happen, but look at all the bad it's brought to people in the world.

Anyways, I hope you guys all go out there and act like givers. Givin' away your time. Your friendship. Even your money. I'm Joe from Winnipeg. Meegwetch.

Feelin' Good

Hey you guys, I'm Joe from Winnipeg. Today I'm gonna be talkin' to you 'bout feelin' good. Man oh man, what's goin' on with politics these days, eh? I heard somebody say to me that it's not about the parties anymore, it's about the job. And the pension. Well, that's not very encouraging, how are we gonna know how to get outraged by the extremes if everyone's sittin' on the fence? Anyways, feelin' good. Well, kind of a strange thing for me to be talkin' about today, but it's what I wanted to try and do for you guys. Make you all feel good. 'Cause a horrible thing happened in our community. Very troubling. The death of a little girl. Now the reason I'm talkin' about this is because I think we need to remember it a little bit longer, before we empty it from our minds with the rest of the painful, awful things we don't want to think about. When I heard of this happening in Winnipeg I was deeply saddened. Shocked. Horrified. Angry. All the emotions most of us who heard this story felt. And a number of people have been tellin' me that they cried when they heard of it. I tried many ways myself to deal with it and still find I'm quite bothered by it. I was thinkin' things like, these are obviously people who are not well and need help. And I understand the mother is a young mother, not much more than a child herself. I even hear some people sayin', well, if they're young enough to make babies, they're old enough to take responsibility. Maybe in some cases, but isn't that like sayin' children who watch television are expected to understand and deal with everything they see on television? They're not obviously, yet many kids watch things they're not supposed to. And then I even thought a bit about what happened to Jack Layton, leader of the NDP, and how he blamed Prime Minister Martin for homeless people dying and some people said, well, homeless people dying is a bit of all our faults. And I thought, that's the case here too. The loss of this young child is all of our faults. You may not agree with that, but I believe we're responsible for our communities and the people in them. And the failures of them. So I thought, you know what, today I'm not really supposed to make people feel good. It's to remind us all that we should feel bad about what's happened. And to use all those negative feelings in a good way, so we make sure things like this don't happen no more. I'm Joe from Winnipeg. Meegwetch.

A Paper Birthday Hat

Hey you guys, I'm Joe from Winnipeg. Today I'm gonna be talkin' to you about a paper birthday hat. I guess I'm gonna vote NDP, I mean Liberal, I mean Conservative, I mean…does it matter anymore? Everybody pullin' a Jean Charest and switchin' parties and everybody puttin' each other down or up, no wonder the Canadian electorate is so confused. It seems more and more we're gonna be voting for the candidate not the party, and maybe that's not such a bad thing. So anyways, a paper birthday hat. Well, with what's been goin' on in the last little while, I've been noticin' a curious thing. History's always being made, sometimes we don't even notice it. But I've seen that some people want to be a part of history, to say, "I was there." I remember when this happened, or that happened. Now I'm talkin' on a grand scale, like what happened on 9-11 or the Transit of Venus. Although that last one has happened millions of times already, we just weren't around to see it. So why are people wanting to be a part of history like this? Don't they know about what Robert Kennedy called an old curse, may you live in interesting times? Doesn't really matter 'cause we live in the time we live in so we may as well make the best of it. And what about bein' a part of our personal histories? Well I've been thinkin' about that a lot. 'Cause see my granny died this week. Oh, I loved her very much. Everybody who knew her did. And I hope you indulge me a little bit, 'cause I know me talkin' about this can be a bit like having to watch somebody's vacation videos, but she was an exceptional person. And when I think of my history with her and the family I was lucky enough to be born into, all I can think of is a picture of my granny from my fourth birthday party. There she is sitting in a paper birthday hat, with one of those curly things that unfurls in her mouth and she's smiling. Having a good time. Having fun. She taught me a lot about what it means to be a human being. How to live and a lot about how to live. Other people. And even yourself. So I hope you guys make some good history today and even if you don't feel it, know that there's love all around you and for you. That's also something my granny taught me. I'm Joe from Winnipeg. Meegwetch.

Solomon's Baby

Hey you guys, I'm Joe from Winnipeg. Today I'm gonna be talkin' to you 'bout Solomon's baby. Hey, did you hear that they lifted the ban on chewing gum in Singapore? It's good to know that important issues involving freedom make the news. But what I really think is goin' on is people get so tired of hearin' or seein' or readin' bad news that the news people feel they have to try and find a way to cheer you guys up. Thing is, they don't seem to do a very good job of it, eh? So anyways, Solomon's baby. Well I guess it's not really Solomon's baby I'm talking about, but kind of what that story represents. That's the one where two women were arguing over whose baby it was, and so King Solomon, who was supposed to be one of the wisest guys who ever lived, said, well, cut the baby in half and you can each have one half. And one woman was horrified at this idea, and Solomon figured out who the baby's mom was. Kind of extreme, but an interestin' way to solve a problem. And it isn't so much the baby I'm thinkin' about, but I am reminded of this horrible story from Ontario, where remains were shipped in the mail. I really hate that I got to keep asking this, but why does this stuff keep happening, and mostly to Native people? I don't know. Anyways, I'm noticin' a lot of elders seem to be leaving us at the moment. And with them goes some of our history and a lot of wisdom. I know that if we listen and remember and tell the stories of our elders that the history lives on, but the people who were there are gone. Here's some wisdom I was told by some elders. Never be afraid to give up your greatest possession. Or any possession for that matter. Listen to your heart. Trust it. And follow it. Do yer best to help others, whether that's doing something for them, talking to them or even just listening. And know that there's more love in the world than hate. I like that last one. Now I'm not gonna say that elders are babies, but you know, just as babies need lots of love, care and attention, so do our elders. And when we take care of them we take care of lots of things, ourselves, our pasts, even our futures. I'm Joe from Winnipeg. Meegwetch.

The Good

Hey you guys, this is me Joe from Winnipeg. Today I'm gonna be talkin' to you 'bout the good. Well, here it is, eh, my last time speakin' to you guys like this. I guess it had to happen sometimes, 'cause all things must come to an end. I will miss you guys. I still remember the first time I talked to you good people, and was I ever scared. Well that's not true, I was freaked out. But you made it so easy for me to talk to you that now I feel very comfortable and just a little sad. So anyways, the good. Well, I have to say chi meegwetch, that's thank you very much for all the linguists out there, I have to say that to my good friend Tom, who gave me the chance to do this. And also thanks to Janice and Kinsey and evrybody else who ever helped me. And of course thanks to you guys for listenin' and talkin' back. And to all my friends and the people who live in rural Manitoba and other parts, remember that you're the living memory of who we are as Canadians. Our past and our future lies in you. So I been thinkin' lots about what I was gonna say today, and I was surprised at how easy it came to me. But then when something's been so good, it's always easy to talk about. And what I want to leave you guys with is somethin' that occurred to me a while back. I was feelin' sad about all the bad we seem to hear in the news all the time. Everywhere you look or hear or read, seems like it's bad somehow. People mistreatin' others. Disrespect goin' on. Even hatred and killing. And I was feelin' a bit overwhelmed by it. Even feelin' powerless and cynical. And I thought, why is the world like this? What's happenin' to us? Why is there so much bad in the world? And what came to me was this…the good. I realized that there is more good in the world. We just don't hear or read or see enough of it. For everyone who is trying to hurt somebody else, or do wrong, there are at least 10 or a 100 more who are doing good, and trying to help. If this weren't true, the world would cease to function if it were filled only with bad stuff. It's because deep down people have it in them. The good. I've seen it in all of you. So don't forget the good that lives in you, and is all around you. It's one of the best things that makes us human beings. And I'm so lucky to have met so many truly good human bein's, who make the earth a better place evry day. I'm just so lucky. Meegwetch to the Creator for lettin' me do this, and thank you to all of you for changin' my life for the better. For teachin' me and showin' me all the good. I'm Joe from Winnipeg. Meegwetch.